Tales of the
Whispering Pines

Tales of the Whispering Pines

J.T. Carruthers

Library of Congress Control Number:		2018903601
ISBN:	Hardcover	978-1-9845-1642-8
	Softcover	978-1-9845-1643-5
	eBook	978-1-9845-1644-2

Print information available on the last page.

Rev. date: 03/23/2018

To order additional copies of this book, contact:
Xlibris
1-888-795-4274
www.Xlibris.com
Orders@Xlibris.com
775908

I dedicate my book to my wonderful husband. I would also like to thank First Editing and Xlibris for all the work that was put into my book. I am truly grateful.

Chapter 1

It was a cold, windy evening in the northern skies of Alaska, where a young father named Christopher Adams and his five-year-old daughter, Sapphire, lived. Their home was deep within the woods of the Whispering Pines. His log cabin was nestled among the fields of wildflowers, streams that sparkled as the sun shone through the trees, captivating mountains, and stars so bright that it would take your breath away. The town was quiet, peaceful, and friendly with a population of about two thousand people.

Chris was a tall brown-haired man with green eyes. He was a handsome, strong-spirited, bearded man who had a warm heart and an adventurous spirit. His most precious gift was his daughter, Sapphire, a pretty little girl with long brown hair, green eyes that sparkled like jewels, and a smile that would warm anyone's heart. Chris was heartbroken when his wife, Samantha, passed away a few months after Sapphire's birth. She was a brave, amazing, and loving woman who chose to stop her cancer treatments to save her unborn child. It was a very difficult time in Chris's life as her memories still stirred in his mind.

Chris was a very busy man. He worked as a tree farmer and a volunteer firefighter. His passion was carving tree trunks into sculptures. He began carving wood after he went to a fall fair a few years back and saw a gentleman creating marvelous works of art with a chain saw, ax, mallet, and chisel. Chris asked if he could train under him to learn his trade. The gentleman named Aaron agreed to train Chris for a month in return for computer lessons to improve his business. This was an easy trade for Chris since he used the computer quite a bit in his business. Chris went to Aaron's house twice a week. It was an exciting time as he learned to use a chain saw to make simple shapes while picking up more advance techniques as the weeks rolled on. In time, Chris was able to move onto more progressive projects like carving wolves, eagles, bears, and owls by the end of the month. Chris realized that if you pay special attention to the small details, the piece would be more pleasing to the eye. He began to carve animals of all sizes, big and small. By the end of the four weeks, Chris felt so grateful that he had the opportunity to learn this art form. Chris continued to practice this new skill and decided that he would sell his carvings as part of his tree business. Aaron thanked Chris for the lessons on the computer and thought that Chris had a special talent for wood carving. Chris wished Aaron the best of luck in his business.

Chris grew up on a farm and always dreamed of having his own tree business. He worked hard to achieve his dream. He went to college and got his bachelor's degree in computer programming, which gave Chris the ability to set aside money to one day own his own tree farm. After graduating, Chris worked for a computer analysis firm in the city. Although he enjoyed his job, he was more excited about his part-time position as a landscape artist in Seattle. It was after five years of saving that he escaped the hustle and bustle of city life. He wanted more freedom to choose something closer to his heart, and that was his love of nature and wildlife. When Chris left his job in Seattle, he chose to live in a small town in Alaska and start a Christmas tree farm with five hundred acres of land. It was a joyful time. This was where he met his beautiful wife, Samantha, while hiking. Their romance blossomed, and they married a year later. The two worked long hours on the tree farm and enjoyed the simple things life can bring. Samantha loved the idea of being surrounded by so much beauty, and moving to Alaska was an easy choice. Growing various types of trees on the farm, cutting, splitting wood to sell, and trimming the trees for the holidays was a blessing. It was a happy time of year that brought so much joy to so many people. Living in the Whispering Pines of Alaska gave Chris a sense of purpose.

The Whispering Pines was a beautiful, tranquil place with a variety of wildlife species and glorious trees. The people in the community were warm, kindhearted, and hardworking. The best part of living in a small town is that everyone looks out for one another. This was why Chris and Samantha decided to raise their family in a small town in Alaska.

Chris had another family member whom he loved, his large white Alaskan malamute named Dakota. Dakota captured his heart the day he rescued her. It was about a year ago when he was hiking out in the woods, looking for dead tree stumps. He began to hear some distant sounds. As he approached, he began to hear the cries of an animal. As he climbed a steep hill and down beyond the open fields, he came across a beautiful puppy in a hunter's trap. He forced the jaws of the trap open. Once released, he carried the injured puppy back to his home. Chris got the dog a blanket and laid her down by the fireplace and called his good friend Jonathan, a veterinarian. Jonathan told Chris that the puppy was a lucky dog. If Chris hadn't found her, she would have died.

"Okay, girl, let's get you cleaned up and see what injuries you have," the vet said. First, he gave the young pup some pain medication, some fluids for dehydration, and then cleaned her wounds around the leg. It took several stitches to close the wound on her leg, and then he bandaged it.

"Does she have a name tag?" Jonathan asked.

"No, nothing. She doesn't even have a collar," Chris told him.

"Well, she needs a name," he said.

"Sapphire and I will take good care of her, and we will name her if no one comes forward to claim her."

"The puppy will need to be on antibiotics and pain medication for a week, and try to keep her from moving around a lot. She needs her rest," the vet told Chris.

"You'll be okay, girl!" Chris said, patting her head. When Sapphire got home from school, Chris told her about finding the puppy. "I've called around, and no one seemed to know who owned this dog. In a month, if no one comes forward, then I guess we'll just have to keep her," Chris said with a smile.

"Yay! I've always wanted a dog!" she said excitedly to her dad.

As the weeks rolled on, no one came forward to claim the puppy. It was a few weeks before the puppy was back to being a fun, loving dog. She received lots of tender loving care while on the mend. She was healing well, and the stitches would be coming out in a few days. Chris told Sapphire that they were adopting the puppy and it was time to name her.

"Well, what would you like to name her?"

"Well, she has beautiful blue eyes so maybe Blue Eyes or Frosty because of her white coat. I know! My teacher once read a story about a wandering homeless German shepherd that was a very brave dog. She heard the cries of the boy and ran toward the sounds. When she saw the little boy splashing frantically, she jumped into the pool. The little boy held on to her back, and the dog swam toward the pool steps. The parents rushed outside and found their son as he was being rescued. The parents were so grateful that they welcomed her into their home. They even had a party to celebrate the dog's brave actions. The little boy named her Dakota, and they became best friends and went everywhere together."

"I like that name," Chris told his daughter. "All right, little Dakota is her new name." She wagged her tail as if she liked it.

As the Christmas season came upon them, it became a busy time of the year for Chris. Each day, as Sapphire was in school, he and his staff would drive into the woods to cut down various-sized Christmas trees to sell on Chris's property. On Saturday morning, Sapphire played with Dakota while everyone worked, but she did help at times. Sapphire joined her father and carried smaller trees to the truck and passed out the hot chocolate and homemade chocolate chip cookies to all the men. Now Sapphire didn't like carrying the trees so much, but she enjoyed when she could plant new trees in the spring.

As the evening sun was setting, the blue sky turned to a breathtaking array of pinks and purples across the horizon. There was a storm coming, so Chris and his staff decided it was time to pack up the trees. They tied the bundle of trees to his truck and headed home. Chris carefully and cautiously drove his four-wheel Dodge Ram as the storm began. It didn't take long before the storm turned to blizzard conditions. As he drove down through the rough roads, the temperatures began to drop quickly, and it became very slick from the packed snow already on the rocky roads. The farther he traveled, the heavier the snow fell. Large snowflakes began to hit the windshield and became heavier and heavier, making visibility near zero.

Suddenly, Sapphire yelled, "A deer!" Chris slammed on his brake, just as a large buck stood in the road, mesmerized by the headlights. The truck slid into a snowbank.

"It was a close call," Chris said. Sometimes even the best driver can experience the unexpected. Chris and his crew looked out their window and watched as the buck ran across the road and into the woods.

"Wow, I guess we were lucky," said one of his crew members.

"Everyone all right?" Chris asked.

"We're all good," they replied.

"Let's head back to the garage so you can all pick up your trucks and go home," Chris said.

"Sounds good to me," one of his staff members said.

Chris put his truck into reverse, while the staff helped push his vehicle out of the snowbank.

While Chris was driving and passing many homes decorated for the holidays, he was reminded of how much Samantha loved the beauty of the Christmas lights as they sparkled like the stars in the heavens. Decorating the house was a tradition that he and Samantha began and one that Chris promised to his wife that he would continue for Sapphire after she was gone. It was a tough thing to do because his heart wasn't in it. He missed his wife tremendously, but he kept his promise to her to brighten up Sapphire's holiday.

It was a magical time for his daughter and so important to Chris that she could see the beauty of Christmas and how much she was loved. Hanging wreaths on the front windows and beautiful garland with its twinkling white lights that strung around the light poles and fences, when he finished the yard, it looked like a winter wonderland. Sapphire's eyes lit up every year. Chris would also set out the animal carvings that he made from the tree stumps. He didn't believe in wasting any part of the tree. He sculpted bears, foxes, rabbits, turtles, birds, and anything a customer asked for. They were incredible pieces of art. Surrounding the animals were Christmas trees that Sapphire and Paige, the babysitter, decorated with pine cones, peanut butter, birdseed, roped strings of popcorn, cranberries, and suet for the birds. Sapphire felt that it was important to take care of the wildlife too.

The carved animals were also offset with many strands of white lights as well as garland and poinsettias. A few more trees were covered in an array of sparkling colors and ornaments all handmade by Chris's mother.

When they arrived at Chris's home, Sapphire opened the door, and Dakota jumped out of the truck, running through the snow and rolling in it.

"She sure loves the snow!" Sapphire laughed.

"Yes, she does!" her father replied. They called Dakota and went inside to sit by the cozy fire. "What a great job you did helping me today. Thank you, Sapphire!" he said with a smile. "Tomorrow since you have no school, Paige will be here to watch you, while I go to work. I need to get the Christmas trees ready to sell."

Paige was a pretty young woman with blonde hair and blue eyes. She was very sweet to Sapphire, and they had become very close.

"You'll have a good day with her," Chris told his daughter.

Paige was a wonderful storyteller and loved to share fun tales with Sapphire. The one story that intrigued Sapphire the most was the tale of the fairies that lived deep within the Northern Lights. The fairies were busy with granting wishes for children and bringing much happiness. They cared for each child and wanted them to get a little bit of magic in their lives. She also enjoyed the tale of the black female bear and how she cared for a lost child in the woods. The child was hiking with her parents and got lost. This young child of six was so scared until a mother bear came and wrapped its arms around the child, keeping the little one warm. When the bear saw a woman crying for her child, she walked with the child as close as she could to the woman, and then when the child saw his mother, he hugged the bear and ran to her.

"Oh, how I wish that those stories were true," Sapphire told her father.

Sapphire was a happy girl who loved adventures. She would read book after book about magical tales and wished one day for her own magical story.

Paige was also a lovely singer and would sing while Sapphire danced. There was always music in the home. Chris would pull out his guitar and join in. Sapphire thought that Paige had a crush on her dad. Dad saw her as only a good friend. She had been babysitting for Sapphire for a few years since Chris's parents, Amber and Eric, moved a little farther south. They only lived a half an hour away, on the outskirts of the Whispering Pines, so they visit often.

When Amber and Eric retired from the farm, they had opened up a bed-and-breakfast (B and B). They called it Adams's Bed and Breakfast. Amber was a tall woman with brown hair and green eyes. Eric was also a tall man with brown hair with streaks of gray, brown eyes, and a small beard.

Amber and Eric enjoyed meeting new people and bringing family traditions into their B and B. Every day held a new adventure and fun things to do. Sapphire loved her grandparents and got to spend a lot of time with them. They were so supportive of their son and helped him whenever they could. Now that the holidays were coming up, Sapphire got to help her grandmother bake cookies and decorate their B and B. Chris's parents lived in a log cabin with a porch wrapped around their house and a lovely swing to enjoy. The holidays were Amber and Eric's favorite time of the year. They had fifty acres of land that were used for their guests to enjoy different types of activities for each season. During the winter months, guests would have many choices, such as sleigh riding, snowmobiling, snowshoeing, skiing, skating, sledding, and doing campfires with delicious s'mores, songs, and lots of laughter. As Amber and Eric would say, it's just one adventure after another when you live in Alaska.

A new dawn arrived, and Chris got ready to head to work.

Paige arrived as he neared the door. "What do you say that we go shopping for cookie ingredients and bake up a storm?" Paige said.

"Sounds good to me," Sapphire said. "Have a good day, Dad!"

"You too, sweetheart," Chris said. "Come on, Dakota, let's get to work."

"Bye, Paige."

Chapter 2

During the holiday season, families would shop for their tree and then enjoy a stroll through Chris's Christmas displays that surrounded the lot. Chris had carved various Christmas figures made out of plywood. He had a Santa, snowmen, elves, bears, reindeer, and more. He painted them and lit them up with a colorful light display. Chris's staff were there to help wrap the trees and collect the money. Paige and Sapphire would sell the Christmas wreaths and offer hot chocolate and cookies for a personal touch to the customers. As for the wood carving, business was picking up there as well. People really seemed to enjoy the talent Chris had in making them and would purchase the carved animals. It was a very exciting time for Chris.

When Chris was just about to head home from work, dispatch called in over his radio. "Calling all available firefighters to a house fire on Crescent Street," the radio announced.

Chris was always prepared for these calls. His truck was supplied with many of the tools that he might need to fight a fire. When the firefighters arrived, they reported the fire was in the front of the house. The fire truck had already arrived when Chris pulled in. A woman with emerald eyes and long wavy brown hair stood outside with her little blonde-haired, blue-eyed daughter.

"Please save my house," the woman cried to a firefighter.

"Please stay back, ma'am," one firefighter told her as he handed a blanket to each of them.

The hoses were hooked up to the truck, and the firefighters went in to put out the fire. A few of the windows were broken to release the heat from the fire. It took about fifteen minutes to get control of the fire. The living room was ruined with blackened walls. Some of the furniture, curtains, a television, lamps, books, rugs, and toys were also badly damaged. There also was smoke damage to the other rooms.

When the fire chief entered the home, he checked out the rooms. After discussing the safety of the home with the fire marshal, it was concluded that the house was unsafe for the woman and child to reenter. There was a lot of work that was going to be needed before returning home. The fire chief looked at the woman and child and felt bad for them. He had to break the news. Chris approached the woman and child and asked their names.

"My name is Destiny Wright, and this is my daughter, Holly," she said. Holly was clinging to her mother and looked very scared.

"My name is Chris Adams. Are you two all right?"

"Yes, we're fine," Destiny answered as a tear ran down her cheek.

The chief stepped up and introduced himself.

"I'm Chief Stevens."

"I'm Destiny, and this is my daughter, Holly."

"Can you tell me what happened here this evening?" the chief asked.

"I was preparing supper while my daughter was playing in the living room when she saw a spark and black smoke coming from the wall socket. I came running into the living room and saw that there was more smoke billowing out of the socket. I felt the wall, and it was getting very hot, so I called 911. The smell of smoke was getting worse by the minute, so I brought my daughter outside."

"Well, I'm glad that you are not injured."

The chief went on to explain to Destiny that he had some bad news for her regarding their home. "The wiring in your living room was faulty, and the sparks you saw caused the flames. The front part of your house is badly damaged. I'm so sorry, but you can't go back into your house until it is fixed up," he said.

"Oh no!" Holly started to cry. "My toys, my books, and my stuffed animals were in the living room. Where are we going to go?" Holly said.

Chris's heart sank when Holly began to cry, so he went back to his trunk and came back with a stuffed bear for her to hold.

"Holly," Chris said as he knelt, "this little bear needs a hug and some loving. Can you be a big girl and take care of him for me?"

"I'm five," Holly said. "I can do that. I think I'll name him Teddy."

"Thank you for being so sweet to Holly," Destiny said.

"Everything will be all right," Chris said.

Then he listened as Destiny told the chief that she had no family in the area. "My mom lives in Utah, and my father passed away."

"Where's your husband?" the fire chief asked.

"I'm not married any longer. My ex-husband left me and Holly shortly after she was born."

"Sorry to hear that," he said.

Chris watched Destiny and Holly get back into their car to stay warm. Chris had a thought, and he went over to tell them.

"I have an idea," Chris said. "If you are interested, I can give my parents a call. They own a bed-and-breakfast, and they would be happy to put you and Holly up while your house is being repaired."

"I don't want to be a bother," Destiny said as a tear ran down her cheek.

"No bother at all," Chris told her.

"This is so sweet of you. I really appreciate it."

While Destiny and Holly waited, another firefighter came over to them and handed them some hot chocolate from his thermos. "It sure is a chilly night. This should warm you up."

"Thank you!" Destiny said.

As the firefighters waited for the last of the smoke to dissipate, they put their hoses and tools away. Chris took this opportunity to call his parents.

"Hey, Mom, this is Chris."

"Hello, dear. I heard about the fire on the radio. Are you all right?"

"I'm fine. There's a woman and child here that can't go back into their home. The front part of the house is in pretty bad shape, and she has nowhere to go. By any chance, do you have a vacancy available?" Chris asked.

"Why yes. We have one room left. It's a busy time of the year with the holiday coming, but for this woman and her child, your father and I would be happy to put her up as long as she needs. She can stay in the cardinal room."

"That's great news. Thanks, Mom! I'll tell her."

Chris walked to the car and told Destiny that she and her daughter had an open invitation to stay at the inn.

"Oh, thank you so much!" Destiny replied.

Once everything was settled, Chris had Destiny follow him to his parents' B and B. It was about ten miles away from Destiny's house, and this gave Destiny a chance to take in this whole situation. She was thinking about all the calls that had to be made in the morning. In the meantime, she thought she would just have to make it through the night.

Chris opened the car door of her blue Mustang and helped them out. Chris's parents were waiting for them to arrive. It was a warm welcome.

"Hi. I'm Amber, and this is my husband, Eric."

"Hello. I'm Destiny, and this is my daughter, Holly."

"Let's put you girls by the fireplace," Amber said with a warm smile. "How about hot cider, a few sandwiches, and some homemade banana bread?" Amber asked.

"That sounds great," Destiny said. "We never did get to eat our supper. Thank you for letting us stay here. You are so kind."

"Chris, you need to shower," Amber said, "and then you can show our guests to the cardinal room." Amber told them that she had some extra clothes that she stored in case visitors forgot to pack enough for their trip. "There's a shower down the hallway from your room so you and Holly can shower," Amber said.

It was getting very late and time to get some sleep. Chris showed them their room and then went home.

"Breakfast is at eight o'clock, so I'll come by and check on you," Chris said.

"Thank you again. Good night," Destiny said. Destiny and Holly showered and went to bed.

As the sun shone through the window, Destiny was still awake, thinking about the fire. Holly woke up and cuddled with her mom.

"Good morning, sunshine," Destiny said.

"Mommy, look at this pretty room. It has a pretty comforter with cardinals and soft red pillows," Holly said.

"It's a very lovely room," her mother said.

"I know how much you love cardinals, Mommy," Holly said.

"Yes, I do."

"Are you okay, Mommy? You look sad."

"Everything will be fine."

"What about all the things that caught on fire?" Holly asked.

"Don't you worry," Destiny replied as she gave Holly a big hug. "Let's go downstairs and have breakfast," Destiny said.

"Good morning! I'll bet you're hungry this morning," Amber said.

"We sure are." Holly spoke out.

"There's pancakes, scrambled eggs, bacon, home fries, pastries, juice, and hot drinks," Amber said.

"Mommy, look at all this food," Holly said.

"Let's dish up and have a seat," Destiny said to Holly. There were other visitors enjoying their breakfast too.

"Hello. It's a beautiful day," Eric voiced as he walked into the dining room. Everyone was so friendly. It was a nice way to start their busy day.

"Hey, Mom," Chris said as he walked into the kitchen. "It's smells good."

Eric went over to his son and asked, "How's the tree farm business?"

"Busy as ever," Chris said. "Good morning, everyone."

"Hi, Destiny. Good morning, Holly," Chris said as he sat next to them.

"I just want to thank you and your parents again for all your kindness last night," Destiny said. "I am taking the day off from work today, so I can call my insurance company. Will I be able to get some of our things out of the house today?" Destiny asked Chris.

"I will call my chief and clear it with him first, and then we'll head out." Chris made the call, and he was cleared to get some of her things out of the house.

"I just want some of my personal things from the bedroom," Destiny said. "I will make a list of items for you," Destiny said.

"Most of your things will smell of smoke and will have to be washed or thrown away," Chris said. "I did notice that your stove, refrigerator, glass table, and cabinets were blackened, but I think that with a good scrubbing, they would be all right. If they don't clean well, then you'll have to get new ones."

"I'll go to the store and pick up some new clothes for a few days while taking care of the clothes that need washing," Destiny said to Chris.

Amber suggested that Holly stay with her and bake some cookies. Holly, still holding her teddy, smiled and said, "I would like that very much." Then Eric offered to get Sapphire so the girls could play. Sapphire was at home with Paige.

"They are, after all, the same age," Chris said.

"What a nice idea!" Amber said. "The girls will have a lot of fun, and you two can get some things done." Amber continued.

"Thank you so much, and breakfast was delicious," Destiny said to Amber.

"Let's head out," Chris said. He continued, saying, "I will go in your house and gather some of your things. Once we have some of your items, we can sort things out."

"May I ask you why you're being so helpful to me? You don't even know me," Destiny asked Chris.

Chris replied, "I know if my home and my daughter were in the same situation as you are, then I would want help too."

"There are so many people who have shown us such kindness that it warms my heart," Destiny said.

"You'll get through this, Destiny," Chris said.

When they arrived at the house, Chris gathered the things on her list, and then Destiny called her insurance. Even her insurance company was kind and understanding. Destiny was told that she would receive her settlement within a week and they would pay her and her daughter to stay at a hotel. Destiny told them about the bed-and-breakfast and the kindness they received. Things were coming along smoother than

Destiny thought. When Destiny received her insurance money, she would hire a contractor to begin repairing her damaged home.

Meanwhile, back at the B and B, the girls had met and were having a great time laughing and being silly and had flour all over their faces and clothes you'd think they were the cookie. Once Amber cleaned them up, the girls went into the toy box and played with some dolls by the warm fire.

"Why don't we go for a hike?"

"It's a beautiful day for a hike," Chris said. "Are you up for it?"

"What a nice idea! The fresh air would be great," Destiny said.

"I know a wonderful trail we can take. You'll love it!" Chris said.

Chris took a pair of snowshoes and poles out of his truck, and he helped Destiny put hers on. Then the hike began. The trail was covered in snow, but the hike was enjoyable. The hike brought Chris and Destiny to the top of the mountain.

"Let's take a little detour. I want to show you something," Chris said. "Come this way, but be careful. We're almost there."

When they reached the crest of the hill, they sat. The view from the top was spectacular. The snow cascaded over the trees, and the snow-covered ground sparkled. It was breathtaking. Chris and Destiny sat on a large rock and just admired the sight. Suddenly, a bald eagle flew by them.

"Wow, they're so big and so beautiful," Chris said.

"Look how they just glide through the air. It's amazing," Destiny said. Changing the subject, she said, "Chris, I am so worried about Holly and our house. How could this happen so close to Christmas?" she asked.

"I know that you're upset, and I would be too, but things will work out. You'll see," Chris answered. "There is always something good that comes out of a tragedy. Just take it one day at a time." They sat on the rock in the quiet for some time before Chris announced, "Let's head back down."

Once they got back on the trail, Chris picked a handful of snow and threw it at Destiny.

"Hey, not fair! I didn't have any snow," Destiny said, laughing.

The snowball fight commenced, and laughter filled the air. Destiny found a good place to hide behind and kept those snowballs flying at Chris. Suddenly, Chris slipped while running toward her.

"Oh no, you don't," Chris said as he ran right into her, knocking her down. They were both laughing so hard.

"I'm sorry. Are you okay?" Chris asked.

"I'm fine. You have quite a throw," Destiny replied with a smile. Chris went to pick her. As their eyes met, the loneliness of Chris's heart softened. Chris helped her brush the snow off her jacket. They were both laughing. "I'll get you next time!" Destiny remarked. Destiny gave Chris a smile, and they both stood there, wondering what to do next.

Chris finally spoke up and said, "You're beautiful."

"Thank you," she replied. Chris's heart was beating so fast, especially when he looked at Destiny. He hadn't felt like this in a long time. He felt scared and wondered if he could feel anything for another woman again. "You know I feel so much better after this hike," Destiny told Chris.

"I'm so glad," Chris replied.

Chapter 3

"So tell me about yourself," Chris said.

"First and foremost, I am a woman with the most incredible daughter. Holly grounds me and makes me enjoy the little things life brings. I am so blessed to have her in my life. I was twenty-one years old when I had Holly. Her father decided that he didn't want to be a dad, so he left. I haven't seen or heard a word from him in the last five years."

"I'm so sorry," Chris said.

"It's all right," Destiny said. "I have been raising an amazing little girl, and I'm so proud of her. Some other things about me is that I love cardinals! They're my favorite bird. I'm a floral designer, and I specialize in designing Christmas trees and wreaths. On several occasions, I am asked to go into people's homes and design something that reflects who they are. I love my job! I have a wonderful mother named Virginia, who has helped me over the years with Holly. I am so blessed. My mother lives in Utah. My father, his name was Albert. He was a good man and my best friend. We did so much together, and Holly was his little princess. He died a few years ago from an automobile accident. I really miss him."

"So sorry, Destiny," Chris said.

"Thank you," Destiny said.

"What's the most favorite tree you ever decorated?" Chris asked.

"I was once asked to design a tree for a youth center. They asked me to design a tree that would reflect the teens' heritage. So I made the theme 'Children around the World.' The tree was placed with many small dolls dressed from their native countries. Since the youth came from different ethnic backgrounds, I thought that would be a great idea. They loved it!" Destiny voiced.

"Nice!" Chris said with a smile. Chris was really beginning to like Destiny, but he was also very nervous.

"Now you know a little about me, tell me about yourself," Destiny said.

"Well, the same as you were saying. My little girl, Sapphire, is my life. She has a beautiful spirit and is full of energy. She helps me on Saturday and Sunday afternoon. She keeps me and my staff in line while we sell our Christmas trees and wreaths. She's quite a character. I work on a five-hundred-acre tree farm. It's my passion to trim the trees and prepare them for the holiday season. I split firewood for my customers. In the spring, I plant new saplings with Sapphire. She loves to plant new life in the soil. It certainly keeps me busy. I also like to do wood carving of animals. It's my hobby. I have the best job ever!" Chris said.

"I would love to see them sometime," Destiny said.

"You already know that I'm a firefighter, but that is only as a volunteer."

"You are an amazing person, Chris," Destiny voiced.

Evening was upon Chris and Destiny as they got back to the truck and headed back to the bed-and-breakfast.

"Hi, girls!" Chris said.

"Daddy, you're here!" Sapphire said, running to him.

"What are you two up to?" Destiny asked as Holly ran up to hug her mother.

"We've had such a fun day. We baked cookies, played in the snow, making snow angels, and now we're resting, having some hot cocoa," Sapphire said.

"Imagine that, they're tired," Chris said with a laugh.

"Holly," Destiny said, "it looks like you've made a good friend."

"She's my best friend," Holly said.

"She's mine too," Sapphire announced.

"Aww. That's nice," Amber said. "Why don't you two go wash up? Supper is almost ready," Amber asked.

Once everyone was seated, Eric gave the prayer of thanks. "Dear Heavenly Father, we thank Thee for this day and for all the beauty that surrounds us. We thank Thee for the blessing of having such a wonderful family being healthy and strong. We thank Thee for the warmth and safety of our home. We ask Thee for peace, comfort, and joy during this holiday season and a special blessing for Destiny and Holly. May the grace of their hearts be comforted in knowing that things will work out. Amen. Let's eat!" Eric said with a smile.

"Your father and I," Amber said, "have decided to put on a Christmas party here at the B and B barn. I'm calling it the Mistletoe Dance. We will have live music from a country band. There will be plenty of food, hot chocolate, a pie-eating contest, face painting, a craft table, a snowman building contest, a bonfire with s'mores, and dancing."

"Daddy!" Sapphire said excitedly. "Can we enter the snowman contest?" Sapphire asked.

"We sure can," her dad replied.

"How would you like to join us in making the best snowman ever?" Chris asked Holly.

"That would be fun," Destiny replied. "I can also help in any other way I can."

"Great! I could use all the help I can get," Amber said.

Once breakfast was over, Destiny and Holly left for the florist shop. Holly was homeschooled, so she would do her studies there.

"Now that Destiny and Holly are gone," Amber said, talking to Chris and Eric, "this Christmas event is going to raise money to help Destiny get back on her feet. She's going to need to replace some of her furniture and some personal items that she lost in the fire. So hush. It's a surprise." Amber said, "I have started a chain for the town to spread the news about the dance, and everyone is so excited. Destiny and Holly will be very surprised. What do you say that we start decorating the house starting with the Christmas tree?"

"I can bring a tall blue spruce home with me tonight, and we can all decorate it this evening. I'm sure Destiny and Holly would love to help along with the visitors," Chris said.

"Sounds good," Amber said. She smiled as she noticed a change in Chris when he talked about Destiny.

"Sapphire, can you go and play for a bit before I take you to school?" her dad asked.

Once she left the room, Amber said, "I have the feeling that you are beginning to like Destiny. Am I right?"

"You know after Samantha passed away," Chris said, "I never thought that someone could warm my heart the way Destiny does. I will always love her and will have a special place in my heart for her. I am so grateful for Sapphire in my life, but there are times when I feel so lonely."

Eric came over and put his arms around his son and said, "Maybe it's time to move on. Samantha would want you to be happy. It's been five years." Just then, Chris was thinking about the hike he and Destiny went on.

"Just take things slow because you have to think of Sapphire, Destiny, and her daughter too," his mother told him.

"Holly is a pure gem, and I like her very much. I know that Sapphire likes Holly too," Chris said.

"Oh, and by the way, before I forget to tell you," Amber said. "Your brother, Daniel, is coming home for the holidays. I know that you two don't see eye to eye, but maybe you can put it aside so we can all have a merry Christmas."

Chris left to bring Sapphire to school, and he headed for work. It was a typical busy day of cutting trees down, making wreaths, and getting them ready to sell, but Chris loved it. As the day turned into evening, he finished his work and went to spend some precious time with Sapphire.

"Hey, princess, I'm home," Chris voiced.

"Daddy! Daddy! I have something to tell you!" Sapphire said excitedly. "My school is doing a project on Saturday mornings for the month of December where a child reads to a dog in a shelter." Sapphire asked her dad if she could be in the school program to help animals get adopted. Her teacher explained that reading books to the dogs makes them calmer, friendlier, and more approachable and makes adoption more likely.

"What a wonderful thing to do for the dogs! Of course, you may be a part of this program," Chris said. "I'll tell you what, I will make a small carved dog for the shelter, and they can raffle it off." Chris continued.

"Awesome idea, Dad!" Sapphire said. "Can I ask if Holly would want to do this with me?"

"Sounds like a good idea," her father said.

When Sapphire called Holly, she got very excited about helping at the shelter.

"Ask your mom if you can come with me," Sapphire said.

"My mom loves the idea and said that I could do the program too," Holly said. "She also said that she would bring us as long as your dad says it's all right." Holly continued.

"My dad loves the idea and said to tell your mom thank you for bringing us to the shelter," Sapphire said.

"Do you think that they would like some donated blankets for the dog?" Holly asked.

"My teacher said that if anyone has any donations, like blankets, toys, or food, it would be great to help out the shelter," Sapphire said.

"My mom makes blankets for children's hospitals, but I know she would love to make some blankets for the dogs," Holly said.

"That's great!" Sapphire said excitedly. "So I'll see you Saturday morning," Sapphire said to Holly.

"Bye!" Holly said.

While Destiny was finishing up on her day, she received a call from the mayor, asking if she would decorate a tree in the town hall.

"Of course, I'd be happy to. What theme would you like?" Destiny asked.

"I think that a patriotic theme would be nice. It would be our way of showing our support for our soldiers," the mayor said.

"I'll tell you what, I will decorate a writing table on the side of the tree for anyone that wants to write a letter to a soldier. I will collect them all by the third week of December and mail the letters out before Christmas," Destiny said.

"That's a great idea, especially being the holiday season," the mayor replied.

After work, Destiny and Holly headed back to the B and B. When they walked into the house, everyone was getting ready for dinner.

"Good evening, ladies. I hope you're hungry," Amber said.

"I sure am," Holly said.

"Where is Eric?" Destiny asked.

"He went to the airport to get our son Daniel," Amber stated. "When Eric and Daniel get back, we are all going to decorate the tree. Chris will be bringing a tree home from his farm." Destiny's heart jumped a beat for joy when she learned that Chris was coming. She was really starting to like him.

"Merry Christmas, everyone! I have come bearing a gift," Chris announced.

"Yay, the tree is here!" Holly said as he carried the tree and set it up in front of the large bay window in the living room.

"It's beautiful!" Sapphire said.

"I love the blue spruce," Eric said.

"The meal is ready, so let's eat. It's finger foods tonight, so we can decorate while eating."

Everyone was so excited as the room was filled with visitors enjoying decorating the tree with garlands, lights, ornaments, and tinsel and hanging their Christmas stockings over the fireplace mantel. They continued putting garlands around the stairs and draping it around the living room. What a beautiful sight. Everyone gathered together as Chris was going to turn on the Christmas tree lights.

"Everyone ready?" Chris asked. "Three! Two! One!" Chris plugged in the lights.

"It's beautiful!" Sapphire said.

"It's awesome!" Holly said. Everyone smiled and cheered.

"Okay, everyone!" Chris said as he brought out his guitar, and they all began singing Christmas carols.

"Hey, Chris," Destiny said. "Tomorrow I have to decorate the town hall Christmas tree and then off to the children's hospital to put up a Christmas tree for the children. Would you like to come and bring your guitar?" Destiny asked.

"I think that sounds like fun," Chris said.

"Hello, everyone!" Chris's brother, Daniel, said as he suddenly walked into the house to give his mother a hug. "Now that I'm here, we can start the fun!" he said with a chuckle.

Daniel's father put his hand on his shoulder with a big smile. Daniel was a muscular man with brown hair and brown eyes. He loved to play tricks on people, especially his brother. He also had a lot of energy. Daniel turned to his brother.

"How are you?" Chris asked.

"I'm great," he said as he walked up to Chris and shook his hand.

"Merry Christmas, brother," Chris said.

"And who's this lovely lady?" he said with a wink to Destiny.

"This is Destiny and her daughter, Holly," Chris said.

"Lovely to meet you, my dear," Daniel said with a kiss to her hand and a smile to Chris.

"Uncle Daniel!" Sapphire said, running up to him. "It's nice to see you!"

"I brought you something," Daniel said as he handed her a gift bag. Sapphire opened the gift and found some small snowballs.

"They're so cute! Thank you!" Sapphire said to her uncle.

"You can play with the snowballs, and they will never melt," he said to Sapphire with a chuckle.

Chris picked his guitar, and Daniel joined in on the singing. The caroling continued until well into the evening. Amber realized how late it was and brought the festivities to an end. As everyone packed up their things, everyone wished one another a good night.

"It was a great night," Destiny said to Amber. "Thank you."

"I'll stop by again tomorrow to see you," Chris said to Destiny.

Chapter 4

The next morning arrived as Chris went to the B and B.

He said, "Good morning, everyone!"

Destiny said, "Good morning," with a smile as she walked into the kitchen. "I'm so glad that you have decided to come help me to decorate the town Christmas tree," Destiny said to Chris. "I'm going to have Holly stay with a babysitter so I can get my work done."

"Sapphire is in school, and then Paige will watch her," Chris said.

"Let's go to the florist and get all the supplies for the trees and put them into my car," Destiny said with a smile. They hopped into Destiny's Mustang and headed out.

Destiny and Chris arrived at the florist and got all the supplies before heading to the town hall.

"The theme for this tree will be patriotic, and I'm calling it Heroes among Us. I asked the mayor for some soldiers' photographs to hang on the tree. I have red, white, and blue ribbon, toy soldiers, flags, gold stars, drums, and horns. I also have to set up a table for people to write letters to our soldiers."

The tree was already set in place so the decorating could begin. As they decorated the tree at the town hall, they laughed and sang Christmas songs. The tree came out wonderful and very patriotic.

"The mayor will be very happy," Destiny announced.

Just as Destiny was putting on the final touch of a soldier on top of the tree, she slipped on the ladder step and was falling. Chris caught her.

"Lucky for me that I have a firefighter around to rescue me," Destiny said as she lay in his arms and smiled.

"Just a lucky catch," Chris said with a chuckle.

Destiny gave him a hero's kiss on the cheek, and Chris smiled.

Once they finished the tree, Chris and Destiny sat and picked a pen and paper and began to write a soldier a letter.

Merry Christmas!

I wanted to write you and thank you for your service. I feel so grateful that you are helping to protect our country. It is with great gratitude that I write you this letter knowing how much your service means to me and so many others. I know that the holidays are difficult being so far from home, but the day will come when you can come home and celebrate with your family.

God bless you and your fellow servicemen during this holiday season, and may the peace, comfort, and joy fill your hearts till we celebrate your return.

Sincerely,
Destiny Wright

Hello from Alaska!

It's a cold time of the year, and I'm hoping that you are well. It is with a humbled soul that I write you this letter. I wanted you to know just how much I appreciate your service to our country. It must be difficult being deployed so far from home, but know that so many care about you and your safety. I will pray that you will return home soon from active duty. I honor you and have much respect and gratitude for you. Thank you.

Merry Christmas!
Chris Adams

As Destiny and Chris finished their letters, they sealed the letters into the envelopes and put them into the mailbox.

"Are you ready to go to the hospital?" Destiny asked.

"I sure am," Chris said.

On the way to the hospital, Chris told Destiny about his brother, Daniel. "He has always been a joker, causing all kinds of mischief when he was young, some were very funny and some not so funny where he'd get punished. Being that I'm the elder brother, he played pranks on me like hiding my homework, misplacing some of my sports gear, or telling the girls stories that weren't true. As he got older, he became more jealous of the direction my life was taking. I tried to coach him and be a good brother, but he wanted to do his own thing. I worked hard in my life to get the things I've wanted. Daniel wanted to have what I had but was not willing to do the work for it. I have asked him to work on the tree farm, but he says that it's not the kind of work he wants to do. So now he doesn't talk to me much, and it saddens me. Maybe this Christmas, we can sit down together and settle things.

"I noticed when he kissed your hand, he winked at me, so I know he's up to something."

"I'm so sorry to hear this. I will pray for you and your brother to reconcile your relationship," Destiny said. "And don't worry about that kiss on my hand. I only have eyes for you," Destiny said.

Destiny was shocked that she said that out loud. But Chris smiled, and Destiny blushed.

Afternoon was approaching as they finished picking up the extra supplies and headed to the hospital. On the way to the hospital, Chris asked, "So what theme is this Christmas tree going to have?"

"I'm calling it Toyland, and there will be all kinds of festive animals, toy soldiers, mini dolls, other toys, colorful garlands, and small plastic balloons."

"This sounds great!" Chris said.

When the two got to the children's hospital, again, the tree was already set in place. Destiny and Chris began to decorate when the children came out of their rooms. The children were being silly, laughing, and wanting to touch the ornaments before they were hung.

It was really adorable. Destiny even let the children hang up a few of the ornaments. Once the tree was finished, Destiny passed out candy canes to each child, and Chris went and got his guitar, and the children began to sing Christmas songs.

"What a gift it is to bring so much joy to the children. It melts my heart watching them, and it was a nice way to end our day," Destiny said.

"Thank you for inviting me. I had a wonderful day," Chris said.

"It was really a fun day!" Destiny said.

When they got into Destiny's Mustang, he leaned over and gently gave her a sweet kiss on her cheek. Destiny blushed but liked it.

"I'll bring you to your truck so you can head home," she said.

Once Destiny went back to the B and B, Chris went to his truck. He was hoping that Destiny liked the kiss. He didn't want to be too forward.

"Good night, Destiny," Chris said.

"Good night, Chris," Destiny repeated with a smile.

"Thanks for the ride," Chris said. "It's been a long day," Chris announced, "but a great one."

As he headed to the bathroom to change, he looked into the mirror and stared at his thick dark beard. He began to think, *Maybe I've had this beard for so long because I was hiding from the world with my sadness when I lost my wife. I know that she wants me to be happy as do I, but it scares me too. I need to believe in myself. That there are good things awaiting me and that I need to take the steps for my own happiness. It is time that I take charge of my life and open my heart to love again. I have not felt so alive as I feel now when I'm with Destiny. She likes me for who I am, and that means the world to me. I think it's time to shave my beard off and clean up.* Again, Chris stared at his bearded face and began to slowly shave off the beard. *This feels right,* he thought.

Once he finished, Chris just stared at himself, thinking how different he looked. *A new man,* he thought with a nod. When Chris came out of the bathroom, he was greeted by his daughter.

"Who are you?" Sapphire asked. "Daddy, it's you! I didn't recognize you. You shaved off your beard. You look so handsome!" Sapphire stated as she touched his face.

"Thanks, sweetie!" Chris replied with a smile. "It's going to take a while to get used to it."

"Wait till Grandma and Grandpa see you!" she said with a smile.

"Sapphire, what do you say that you get ready for bed and I'll read you a story?" Chris read Sapphire a Christmas tale and then tucked her into bed.

"Daddy, did you have a nice day with Destiny?" Sapphire asked.

"Yes, I did. I had a wonderful day decorating Christmas trees," Chris said.

"I like her very much," Sapphire said.

"I like her too," Chris said.

"Do you ever think of Mommy?" Sapphire asked.

"I loved your mother, and she will always have a special place in my heart. Every time I look into your beautiful green eyes, I see your mother."

This made Sapphire very happy as she gave her dad a big hug.

"Good night, Sapphire," her father said.

"Sweet dreams, Daddy," Sapphire responded.

The day arrived when Destiny brought Sapphire and Holly to the dog shelter to read to the dogs. It was an exciting time as the girls found a book and a few crocheted blankets that Holly's mother made for the shelter dogs to sit on. The girls sat outside of the dog crates and began to read. Holly sat next to a mixed breed and began reading. Sapphire read to a Dalmatian. Reading to the dogs was a very rewarding experience for the two. They read two to three stories to a few of the other dogs. What was really interesting was how shy the dogs were in the beginning, but by the time the girls finished reading, the dogs would be lying next the them, wagging their tails.

"Okay, girls, it's time to head home," Destiny said.

"We'll see you next week," Holly said with the kiss blown from her hand to the puppies.

"Me too, puppies," Sapphire said.

"I'm glad you both had a great time. Time to head back to the bed-and-breakfast," Destiny said.

When Chris got to his mother's house after work, he walked in, and everyone was surprised at his new look.

"Look at you!" Chris's mother said, touching his smooth face. "No beard. I think someone is trying to impress a young lady," she whispered in his ears.

"Mom!"

"It looks nice," Amber said.

"Thanks, Mom," Chris replied. "I thought it was time."

"Now you don't look like a bear," Daniel said.

"Funny, bro," Chris replied.

When Destiny, Sapphire, and Holly returned to the B and B, Chris, Eric, and Daniel were decorating the front yard with garlands, strings of lights, and hollies. An old-fashioned red sleigh rested in the front yard, adorned with lights, hollies, and wrapped presents. A wreath on the front of the sleigh with a big red bow was the perfect touch. The yard was also adorned with a reindeer, penguins, polar bear, and angels. They were a sight to see as they all lit up and moved gracefully.

"Looking good, Dad!" Sapphire announced. When they finished the decorating, all the men went in and enjoyed a cup of hot cocoa.

"It's so nice to see my family sharing the joy of Christmas. The yard looks very festive. Good job, gentlemen," Amber said with a smile.

"Thanks, honey," Eric said with a kiss to his wife's cheek.

"So how was your day at the shelter?" Chris asked the girls.

"It was so much fun!" Sapphire said.

"I can't wait to go back again. The dogs are so cute!" Holly replied.

"Thanks for taking them, Destiny," Chris said with a smile.

"You're welcome," Destiny replied. Destiny whispered in Chris's ear that she liked the new look.

Destiny excused herself and said, "Holly and I are going to go to our room to rest, and we'll see you soon."

"Okay, we'll see you later," Amber said. "We need some wood for the fireplace," Amber said to her sons. "Would you two go get me some?"

"Sure," Chris replied.

The brothers went outside and began to split some wood for the fire.

"Daniel," Chris said, "can we talk?"

"About what?" Daniel replied in a distant voice.

"Why after all these years can't we be friends?" Chris asked.

"You know," Daniel said, "you always get everything you ever wanted, while I worked hard trying to show others that I'm just as good a person you are. Things always come easily to you."

"Are you kidding me? I worked my butt off trying to succeed in life. I studied hard, worked to make a career for myself. Nothing came easy," Chris said.

"You even had the best wife," Daniel said.

"Is this what all of this is about!" Chris said in a loud voice. "Yes, I had a wonderful wife, and I miss Samantha very much, but it's time that I move on."

"With Destiny," Daniel said.

"If that is in cards for me, then yes," Chris said. "I want you to be happy, and I will do whatever I can to help you, Daniel."

"Well, I've been doing pretty well on my own," Daniel replied.

"That's great!" Chris said.

"Let's just finish getting the wood for Mom," Daniel said.

The two brothers split enough wood for the house with some extra and brought it inside.

"Thanks, boys," Amber said. "There's nothing like a toasty fire to set a happy mood."

"I think that I'll go snowshoeing," Chris said to his parents. "Can you watch Sapphire for me?" he asked his mother.

"Sure," she answered. "Have a nice hike, but be careful. It's going to be getting dark soon."

Chris went up the mountain to his favorite spot overlooking the beautiful valley of the trees below. He felt that he needed to do some thinking about his brother and what he could do to straighten it out. Chris also needed to make a big decision about the idea of opening his heart to the possibility of falling in love again. When he got back from his hike, Chris asked his mother and father if they could talk.

"Let's go sit at the table," Amber said with his father following.

"I am so saddened by Daniel always feeling as though he has to compete with me. I don't know what to do," Chris said.

"It's up to Daniel to decide how he wants to live his life. He hasn't seen you in a few years. Just give him time to see you as a dad and how good you are as a parent. His eyes may open. Maybe when he sees how happy Sapphire is, he'll see that you're a nice guy and that he doesn't have to compete with you," Eric told Chris.

"I also have feelings for Destiny. Do you think that I'm moving too fast?"

"Your heart is telling you to embrace life and all it has to offer you," his mother said. "Destiny coming into your life was no coincidence. It was fate. Samantha would want you to be happy, and this is your opportunity for reaching out and following your heart."

"What about Sapphire?" Chris asked.

"Sapphire wants you to be happy. Maybe you should talk to Sapphire first."

"Let her know how you feel about her," his father said, "and also how you feel about Holly."

"I will, Dad. Thanks, Mom. Thanks, Dad. I always feel better after we've talked," Chris said with a kiss to his mother's cheek. "Thanks for listening."

Chris went into the living room to get Sapphire. He put her on his lap.

"You know, sweetie, I wanted you to know that I really like Destiny and her daughter. I wanted to be honest with you and let you know."

"Ah, Daddy, I already know. I see it in your eyes when you look at her, and you're so nice to Holly. I want you to be happy, and you deserve it," Sapphire announced.

"Wow, I guess you know me better than I know myself," Chris said with a hug.

"Can I go play now?" Sapphire asked as she saw Destiny and Holly come out of their bedroom.

Amber began working on the Christmas dance. Destiny saw Amber working on something at the table.

"Hello, Destiny," Amber said. "I'm making a chart of where to place the stations. It needs to be organized."

"I'd be happy to help," Destiny said.

"Why don't you and Destiny work on the chart and Chris, Sapphire, Holly, and I will go watch some television?" Eric asked. "I know there's some great Christmas shows on TV tonight."

Right before Chris was about ready to leave, he noticed his brother going over to Destiny and flirting again. Chris walked over and gently took Destiny by the hand.

"Hey, brother, chill out!" Daniel said. "I was just talking to her." But Chris knew better. He still wanted to chase after what Chris wanted.

"I don't want to argue with you, Daniel. I just what you to know that I have feelings for her."

Destiny was so excited to hear this even if he was telling his brother before her. They all began to talk and settled the situation by telling Daniel that he would like to continue to get to know Destiny if that was all right with her.

"Let's go outside, Destiny," Chris said. So Chris and Destiny went out on the swing and started talking.

"It's a beautiful night. The stars are so bright," Destiny said.

"Yes, it is," Chris said. "Destiny, first of all, let me say that I'm sorry I told my brother about my feelings for you before telling you," Chris said.

"I am so happy to hear that you feel that way because I have feelings for you too," Destiny said with a smile.

"I know that you had a bad past with your ex-husband, but I want to give you and Holly the best that I can. I promise to be honest to you and not to disappoint you or hurt you. I want to make this journey extraordinary where all our wishes and dreams come true," Chris said.

"I feel the same way," Destiny replied. "I want you and Sapphire to be happy, and I want to be with you," she said, blushing. "By the way, I'm surprised you shaved off your beard. I like it, but I liked you even if you kept the beard."

"Thanks. I really did it for you. I was hiding behind my beard, and I needed to take charge of my life, and this means with you. So will you be my girlfriend?" Chris asked.

"I would love to!"

"Hey, Destiny, look up," Chris said. "There's mistletoe hanging above us," Chris said as they shared their first kiss. "Let's tell our girls tomorrow," Chris said.

"I know that Holly really likes you, so she'll be thrilled," Destiny told Chris.

"I know Sapphire will be too," Chris announced as he held Destiny close. "Before heading home, why don't we take the girls outside and make some snow angels?" So the two bundled up the girls in their snowsuits and headed outside.

"Let's make some snow angels, girls!" Chris announced, running for the snow.

"I'll beat you," Holly said to Chris.

One by one, the snow angels were made.

"The snow angels are so pretty, especially their wings," Holly said.

"This is fun!" Sapphire said.

"Well, how about we have a snowball fight!" Destiny said as she threw a flying snowball right at Chris's back.

The snowball fight began as swirling snow began to fly around, landing on one another. There was so much laughter that Chris's parents came out and joined the snowball merriment. Even Daniel came out as well and joined in on the fun. It was a wonderful evening, and it was great to do this as a family.

The evening was coming to a close as Chris said, "It was getting late. I need to bring Sapphire home. We'll see you tomorrow, Mom."

"All right, see you then, Chris," Eric said to his son.

"Bye, Daniel," Chris said as he waved his hand. "Good night, Destiny and Holly."

"Good night, Chris, and to you too, Sapphire," Destiny said with a smile.

Chapter 5

Morning came as Sapphire got ready for school.

"When I get back from work tonight, I need to talk to you," Chris told his daughter. "Have a great day!"

"You too, Daddy!" Sapphire said.

When Sapphire got to school, her classmates were all talking about going to the shelter to read to the dogs. Even Mrs. Campbell, the teacher, was thrilled to hear so many stories.

Mrs. Campbell told the children to have a seat and that she had some good news for them. She told them that the shelter called her this morning, reporting that five of the dogs and two puppies were adopted over the weekend. All the children cheered. Mrs. Campbell also said how proud of them she was and that they made a difference in helping those dogs get adopted. The children were so excited. Sapphire told her teacher that she couldn't wait to tell her friend Holly the wonderful news. The school day went by fast. Soon, Sapphire was heading home. Paige and Dakota were there to greet her off the bus.

"Hi, Sapphire," Paige said. "Did you have a nice day at school?"

"Yes, I did!" Sapphire replied as she patted her dog. "Hi, girl." Sapphire said excitedly, "I have some great news to share, but I want to wait till Daddy comes home."

"Well, I can't wait to hear it," Paige told her. "Let's go home so you can get your homework done and take Dakota for a walk."

"All I have is spelling words to put into sentences," Sapphire said. Once her homework was done, Paige and Sapphire brought Dakota for a nice walk. Heading back home, Sapphire saw her dad's truck and ran home. "Come on, Dakota!" she yelled. "Daddy! Daddy!"

Chris pulled into the driveway as Sapphire and Dakota ran down the sidewalk.

"Hey, what's all the excitements?" he asked.

"Come on, Paige! Hurry!" Sapphire yelled.

"My teacher, Mrs. Campbell," Sapphire said in excitement, "told us this morning that five of the dogs and two of the puppies were adopted over this past weekend."

"That's great news!" Chris said, giving her a big hug.

"Congratulations, Sapphire!" Paige said happily.

"When can we see Holly?"

"After supper, we'll go," Chris replied.

"Can we have something quick? I really, really want to tell Holly!" Sapphire said, still very excited.

"We have some leftover macaroni and cheese we can heat up and then head over to Grandma's house," Chris said. "Paige, why don't you come too? It's been a while since you've seen my parents."

"I would like that," Paige answered.

Once supper was finished, they all headed over the grandma's house. Sapphire was so antsy she couldn't sit still. "We're almost there, Sapphire," Chris said. Chris parked his truck, and Sapphire ran inside.

"Hi, Grandma! Is Holly here?" she asked.

"Holly and her mother had some errands to do, and they said they would be back in a little bit," her grandmother told Sapphire. "Hello, Paige, how are you? It's nice to see you," Amber said with a hug.

"It's nice to see you too," Paige said.

"Oh, Paige, this is my son Daniel," Amber said.

"It's nice to meet you," Paige said with a smile. "You look a lot like your brother." Daniel groaned.

"What's all the excitement?" her grandfather asked.

"I'll tell you when they get here," Sapphire said, feeling a little disappointed.

"Look," Chris said, "they're pulling up the driveway now." It wasn't long before Sapphire held the front door open and let them in.

"What's going on?" Destiny asked.

Sapphire said, "My teacher said that because we read to the dogs and puppies, they were very calm and playful. Five people adopted the dogs, and two people adopted two of the puppies." The girls started jumping and in a circle, screaming of joy.

"Congratulations, girls!" Destiny said as she hugged them.

Chris whispered to Destiny, "Now would be the time to tell the girls about us dating."

"Let them enjoy their excitement for a little longer," Destiny suggested.

Chris then thought of a nice way of telling them. Again, Chris whispered in Destiny's ear, saying, "Why don't we all go on a sleigh ride and we can tell them then?"

"What a great idea!" Destiny whispered back to Chris.

Once the girls calmed down, Chris told them, "Destiny and I have something to tell you two. How about we go on a sleigh ride?"

"I'll make you some hot cocoa for the ride," Amber said.

Everyone gathered their coats, hot cocoa, and blankets and headed outside. There was some snow falling, and it made the scene so picturesque. The horse was hooked to the sleigh, and the sleigh ride began. As Chris took the reins, the horse trotted, and there was the jingle of the bells.

"It's such a beautiful night," Destiny said.

"Let's try to catch some snowflakes on our tongue," Sapphire said. What fun they all were having as the ride went around the grandparents' large property. You could see the magic of Christmas everywhere you looked.

Chris said, "Girls, we want to tell you something. We hope that you will like the news. Destiny and I have been seeing each other for a while, and we are going to start dating. We both love you, girls, and want you to be happy for us."

"We will all take our time getting to know one another," Destiny said.

"Well, I think it's great!" Sapphire said. "My daddy deserves to be happy, and I can tell that he likes you a lot."

"Yay, this makes me so happy too!" Holly replied.

"Are we a family?" Sapphire asked.

"I believe that we are becoming a family," Chris said with a smile.

They all cuddled together, feeling much joy and happiness.

"Well, we better get back now and have you girls sit by the warm fire," Destiny said.

When they got back, Daniel and Paige were talking and laughing.

"Hey, Chris! You never told me about this beautiful woman. She's pretty amazing," Daniel voiced.

"She's been a lifesaver for me, caring for Sapphire after school and school vacations. I don't know what I'd do without her," Chris replied.

Paige said, "I enjoy taking care of Sapphire. We're good buddies."

"How about you and me go out for a coffee sometime?" Daniel asked Paige.

"I would like that," she replied, blushing.

"How about tomorrow afternoon?"

Chris thought his brother was sure moving quick. The next day arrived as Paige got ready for her date with Daniel. Daniel picked up Paige at Chris's house just as Chris arrived home from work. When he saw Chris, Daniel said, "I'll take her out and bring her home safely."

"Have a great time," Chris said.

"Bye, everyone," Paige said as she went out the door.

Daniel and Paige went to a coffee shop in the center of town.

"So how long have you been watching Sapphire?" Daniel asked.

"It's been a few years. Since your parents moved away. Your parents are wonderful people. I really like them a lot."

"Thanks. I think they are pretty awesome," Daniel said. "They have always been there for me even when I was getting into trouble."

"So what kind of things did you do?" Paige asked.

"I liked hiding things from Chris, so when he went looking for it, he couldn't find the item. I'd put girl's perfume on his gym clothes or tease him about his girlfriends. It was pretty funny," Daniel said.

"Do you really think that was nice?" Paige asked.

"I was just a kid and liked playing practical jokes on my brother," Daniel replied. "It's just sibling rivalry."

"You know your brother is a good man, and he's raising an amazing daughter. It's not easy for him, but he does his best," Paige said.

"Wow, you really like my brother!" Daniel said.

"I've gotten to know him, and yes, I think he's a great guy," she said.

Daniel felt the jealous bug and got a little annoyed.

"If you like him so much, why did you go out for coffee with me?" Daniel asked.

"He's my boss, and I have respect for him. I think that I should go home now," she said, not feeling comfortable any longer with Daniel.

"All right, I'll bring you home," Daniel replied, annoyed.

The next morning, Paige was helping Sapphire get dressed for school when Chris asked, "How'd the coffee date go?"

"It really wasn't a date. Your brother has some issues, but I think in time, being back home, he will see the light and things will work out."

"You have such a positive outlook on life, and that's why I like you taking care of my daughter."

"Thank you. You're very kind," Paige replied.

"After school, can you bring Sapphire to my mom's house? They're going to be making gingerbread cookies for the charity event and a gingerbread house."

"I'd be happy to," Paige said.

The day went by fast, and Sapphire came home from school. Paige brought her to Amber's house and dropped off Sapphire. When Daniel saw Paige, he walked up to her and apologized to her and said how they left on a bad note. "I know that sometimes I put my foot right into my mouth and say things that are a little unkind," Daniel said. "I'm sorry," he said. "Can we try again? I did a lot of thinking last night, and I realize what a jerk I have been to you and my brother. I know that I get jealous of my brother, but it's time that I start living my own life and not worry about his."

Amber was very pleased when she overheard Daniel's confession and was very pleased that her son was opening up his heart and realizing that his brother wasn't so bad.

Paige accepted his apology and agreed to go out with him again.

"Let's go skating," Daniel told her.

"Sounds nice," Paige replied.

Daniel and Paige went down to the skating rink on his parents' property and got ready to skate. There were white lights strung around the skating rink, hay bales covered with blankets, and decorated trees around the arena. It was simply elegant.

Daniel and Paige enjoyed their time skating and kept the conversation fun and light.

They skated for a few hours and then went back to the B and B. As Daniel and Paige came walking in, Amber asked if they had a nice time. She said, "Hot cocoa is ready and waiting for you if you two need to warm up." Daniel and Paige got their hot cocoa and sat on the floor by the fire.

"Hey, Mom, do you have any marshmallows?" Daniel asked.

"Yes, I think that I do," Amber replied. "Here's the sticks and the marshmallows for roasting. Enjoy!" she said with a smile.

Meanwhile in the kitchen, Amber and Sapphire were baking lots of gingerbread cookies and decorating them. Sapphire wondered why so many cookies and asked, "This is a lot of cookies. What are they for?"

"Destiny suggested a gingerbread-themed tree where people could pick out a scrumptious cookie that they could enjoy. When we're done, we have to wrap in each decorated cookie in a clear baggie and tie them with a red bow so they look pretty for the Christmas tree."

When they finished all the cookies, they started to decorate a large gingerbread house. Amber had prepared all different colors of frosting and an array of red and green peppermint candy, colored round chocolate morsels, red and black licorice, candy canes, gumdrops, different-shaped animals cookies, wafers, and sprinkles to decorate the gingerbread house.

"This is going to be the best gingerbread house ever made!" Sapphire said.

Just as they began to decorate, Destiny and Holly came home from the florist shop.

Sapphire asked them, "Would you like to join in?"

Holly replied, "Yes! This is going to be fun!"

"Thank you for asking us," Destiny said.

It was a few hours before the gingerbread house was finished. It was a large castle with a bridge and decorated to the hilt. It surely was a masterpiece. Everyone really had fun making it. Destiny and Amber carefully carried the gingerbread house to the dining room table.

"We can enjoy the gingerbread here until we decide to eat," Amber said to everyone.

When Eric woke up from his nap, he went looking for Amber and found her in the dining room. "Wow!" he said. "That is a beautiful gingerbread house. Who has this much talent?" he asked.

"We do!" the girls said in unison.

"Well, you two girls are very talented young ladies," Eric said with a big smile. "Now when do we get to eat it?" he asked.

"Let's just enjoy it for a few days. Then we can eat it," Amber said.

"It's just too pretty to eat," Destiny responded.

"It will be just as pretty to eat," Amber said with a laugh.

"I hear a car pulling in. Could it be Daddy?" Sapphire spoke. Sapphire looked out the window and saw Chris's truck. "It is Daddy!" she said excitedly.

As Chris walked into the house, Sapphire and Holly brought him into the dining room to see the gingerbread house.

"Who made the colossal gingerbread castle?" he asked.

"We did!" the girls said in harmony.

"Well, it's beautiful!" Chris said to everyone. Chris turned to Destiny and asked, "How was your day?"

"I've been helping your mom work on some of the theme ideas for the Christmas trees that will be at the mistletoe dance."

Sapphire spoke out suddenly. "Excuse me, but can I go and ask Daniel and Paige if Holly and I can roast marshmallows too?"

"Sure, go ahead," Destiny told them.

"Sure, come on!" Daniel replied.

"Amber," Destiny said, "I have a wonderful idea how we can raise money and have fun decorating themed Christmas tree. Let's have a raffle where people put their raffle tickets in the box in front of the tree they want to win."

"I'll donate ten trees to decorate and raffle off," Chris said.

"That's great, Chris!" Destiny replied with a hug.

"So what kinds of themes should we have?" Chris asked.

"Amber and I have made a list. So far we have ten themes."

Themes Christmas Trees
Poinsettias Christmas
Children's Crafts
Caring
Gingerbread Tree
Angels Watching over Us
Seed of Hope
Vintage Christmas
Comfort and Joy
12 Days of Christmas
Woodland Wonders

"These are all great ideas!" Amber said as she read the list. "I think we should use all of them. I will ask the local retail stores if they would like to donate any of the items for the trees. It's good business sense to show a little of the Christmas spirit," Amber said.

"I'll ask around the florist shop, and I'm sure that my boss would donate some things," Destiny said.

"This is all coming together. I am so happy," Amber voiced.

"Let's go relax by the fire and join Daniel, Paige, and the girls for roasting marshmallows," Amber said.

"Sounds good," Destiny said. Chris took Destiny by the hand and walked into the living room and sat.

Amber brought more marshmallow sticks and passed them out.

"Come join us," Paige said with a smile.

"Thank you," Chris said, reaching for a marshmallow.

When Daniel and Paige were done with the marshmallows, Daniel walked Paige to her car and gave her a kiss good night. When he came back, Chris and Sapphire got ready to go home. But before he left, Chris asked Destiny out on a date. "Let's get all dressed up and go to the Chalet. I'd like to show off my beautiful date."

Destiny blushed and said, "That sounds nice." Destiny thought, *I need to get a new dress.* She was so excited for this date.

"I'll watch Sapphire," Amber said happily.

"See you tomorrow," Chris said. "I'll pick you up at seven. Good night, Destiny," Chris said. "Good night, Holly." He continued and to everyone else.

"Bye, everyone!" Sapphire shouted.

"Good night," Amber said as she and Eric waved goodbye.

"Good night, brother," Daniel said.

On the way home, Chris started telling Sapphire what a nice day it had been, but Sapphire was so tired that she fell fast asleep in the truck.

Chris carried Sapphire to bed and then decided to write Destiny a letter.

> Dearest Destiny,
>   I know that we haven't known each other very long, but I have to tell you how much you have opened my heart. I honestly didn't think such deep feelings would ever embrace my life again. I see that the simple things in your life make you happy and bring you joy. I too enjoy the simple things of life and the happiness it can bring. What I'm trying to say is that I would truly like to continue on our journey and see where it takes us.
>
> Chris

Chris read over his brief letter, and it warmed his heart knowing that he would be able to give it to Destiny tomorrow night. Night passed ever so slowly as it always does when one is excited about an event. Chris worked his day on the farm whistling and singing some tunes. He was excited about his date with Destiny that evening. Before going home, he stopped at a florist to get Destiny some long-stemmed red roses. When he got home, he made supper and got Sapphire settled for the evening. Chris's mother left a message for Chris that she wasn't feeling well, so

Destiny brought Holly over to Chris's house. Paige, Sapphire, and Holly would have a great time all together. Paige decided to stay at Chris's house instead of going home. Paige had the whole evening planned. They were going to play games and dress up, and to top the night off, they were going to make a fort of blankets for their sleepover. Once Paige, Sapphire, and Holly were settled, Chris and Destiny headed out. He thought about the days they shared together snowshoeing, throwing snowballs, and enjoying each other's company on the swing. When Destiny arrived, she was dressed in a beautiful black dress with emerald jewelry around her the neck and dangling from her ears.

"You take my breath away," Chris told Destiny.

"You look pretty sharp too, Chris," Destiny said. Turning to Holly, Destiny told her daughter to have a good night.

"I will."

"Don't wait up for us," Chris told everyone.

When they arrived at the Chalet, candles were lit in the entryway, giving a warm glow and a romantic feel to the evening. As Chris and Destiny entered the restaurant, the hostess greeted them with a warm smile. The restaurant was very elegant with velvet chairs, red tablecloths, candles, and a small floral centerpiece at each table. There was also a woman playing a piano in the corner of the room. The room was lovely and inviting. During their five-course meal, Chris and Destiny enjoyed their conversion, and they had learned so much more of each other. After their delicious meal, a beautiful song was playing, so Chris asked Destiny if she wanted to dance. They held each other close and swayed ever so gently to the music.

"You know I love the piano," Destiny said.

"Do you play?"

"I did as a child, but as I grew older, time got away from me. I am having such a lovely evening. I wish it would never end," Destiny said.

"I have a surprise in store for you. Our night will be perfect," Chris remarked.

As the evening moved on, Chris and Destiny continued to dance into the late hours. The restaurant was getting ready to close, so Chris said, "Remember when I said I have a surprise for you? Well, I'm taking you somewhere. I asked Holly to pack you some warm clothes. So before we leave, we have to change."

"What are you and Holly up to?" Destiny asked.

"You'll see the surprise soon," Chris declared. By the time they arrived, it was two in the morning. He stopped the truck and covered Destiny's eyes with a handkerchief. "Now we are just about there," Chris said. He stopped the truck once again. Chris went over to the side door and helped Destiny out. "Just take my hand, and we'll walk slowly," Chris said. Once they reached their destination, Chris helped Destiny around the rocks.

"Where are we?" she asked.

"You'll see in a moment," Chris said as he let go of her hand, walked a few feet away, and laid a blanket on a bench. "Okay, you can take your blindfold off," Chris said.

Destiny was speechless; it was the northern lights. "I am in awe," Destiny said.

"It's the aurora borealis, and I never tire of seeing these magnificent rays of light," Chris said. "I made this bench so I could come and watch the aurora any chance I can," Chris remarked.

"It's mesmerizing," Destiny said.

"You know," Chris said, "I don't bring many people here, but I wanted to share it with you. You mean a lot to me, Destiny, and I am so happy to have these special moments to get to know you."

"I feel so blessed and grateful that you wanted to share this personal place with me. It means a lot to me," Destiny voiced. Chris and Destiny shared a sweet kiss. "This has been such a wonderful evening. Thank you, Chris."

"You are so welcome, Destiny."

Chris and Destiny stared out at the aurora and enjoyed the peace and tranquility as the waves of color danced about in the sky, watching the northern lights in an array of greens and purples. *It's like looking at a dream. It's so beautiful,* Destiny thought. Chris and Destiny stayed there for what seemed like hours, embraced in the joy of being in the moment. As the evening passed and morning arrived, the sun was rising.

A beautiful sunrise occurred just as they started back to the truck. They walked to the truck hand in hand.

"Before I take you home, I have something for you," Chris remarked.

"What is it?" Destiny wondered.

Chris gave Destiny the letter and asked her not to read it until she got home.

"Okay, I promise I won't."

The two headed back to Chris's house.

"Good morning, you two!" Paige said as she was preparing breakfast.

"Good morning, or should I say good night? I need to get some sleep," Destiny said. Destiny would bring Holly back to the B and B for some rest. "Thanks for watching Holly," Destiny said to Paige. "Bye, Chris," Destiny said with a smile as she headed out.

Once Destiny and Holly arrived back at the B and B, Amber said she was feeling better. She offered to take Holly so she could get some rest. The first thing Destiny did before going to sleep was to read Chris's letter. As Destiny read the letter, a tear rolled down her cheek. She was so happy, and she began to think that Chris may be the one. She had never been treated so kindly and lovingly before. It warmed her heart to know that Chris cared enough for her that he would write this beautiful letter. After reading the letter, she lay down and quickly fell asleep.

"So, Chris, did you two have a great evening?" Paige asked.

"It was magical," Chris said. "I brought her to the Chalet and had a wonderful meal and a lot of dancing until the restaurant closed. Then I showed her the northern lights at my special spot. I could tell that she was in awe of the aurora borealis. The colors were stunning, and movements looked like a dance. I haven't had a night like this in years. I told her that we would take things slow, but I think that I'm falling hard for her."

"You don't take just anyone to your spot, so I know your feelings for her are pure. I'm really happy for you," Paige said. "Destiny is a sweet woman."

Sapphire heard her dad in the house and sat up in bed. Sapphire jumped out of bed to see her dad.

"Good morning, Daddy," Sapphire said.

"Did you have a good evening last night?" Chris asked.

"We had so much fun last night!" Sapphire said. "We painted, played with some puzzles, read some books, played dress up, made up a play, and then made an awesome fort."

"I'm so glad," Chris said. "Sounds like you had as good of an evening as I did."

"Did you have a nice time with Destiny?" Sapphire asked.

"Why don't we sit down and have breakfast and we can talk about it while we eat?" Chris asked.

Paige and Chris continued preparing breakfast, while Sapphire set the table.

"Breakfast is ready," Chris said. "Let's eat!"

Paige and Sapphire listened as he talked about his date with Destiny. When he began to talk about the aurora borealis, Sapphire asked him if he saw any fairies.

"Holly told me about a book she has, and it tells the story of fairies living in the northern lights."

"No, sweetheart, I didn't see any fairies," Chris told his daughter.

Once Chris finished talking about his evening, breakfast was over. Chris thanked Paige for helping him out, and then she went home. Sapphire went to her bedroom and got dressed for the day.

Sapphire came out of her bedroom and asked if she could go and see Holly. Feeling exhausted and exhilarated, Chris brought Sapphire to visit Holly. When Chris arrived at the bed-and-breakfast, Amber knew he was up late and into the morning because Destiny also came home in the morning. Destiny was fast asleep, while Holly was up with Amber.

When Amber saw Chris, she said, "Chris, why don't you go and get some sleep on the couch? I'll take care of Sapphire."

"Thanks, Mom. I'm exhausted. That would be great. A few hours of sleep would do me some good," Chris told his mother.

"Girls," Amber said, "after breakfast, Grandpa and I need to do some shopping for the Christmas dance, and you both can come with us."

"Yay!" the girls replied.

Holly went quietly into her bedroom as to not wake up her mom sleeping and got dressed. Destiny slept for several hours and then was woken up by the ring of her cell phone.

"Hello," Destiny said.

"This is your insurance agent wanting to tell you that there is a check here for you to pick up. Now you can hire a construction company to begin the rebuilding of your home this week."

"This is great news! Thank you so much!" Destiny answered.

Destiny ran into the living room and saw that no one was there but a note telling her where Amber and the girls went. She knew that Holly had probably gone out with Chris's parents. When she turned around, she saw Chris on the couch sleeping. Destiny knelt and whispered into Chris's ear.

"Hey, babe," Chris said as he sat up.

"I have some great news," Destiny said. "I have to go and pick up my insurance check at the insurance agency."

"Well then, let's go!" Chris said.

When they left, they put a note on the table about where they were going. Chris and Destiny drove to the insurance agency, and then they went to talk to a contractor.

"I told you things would work out," Chris whispered in her ear.

The contractor told Destiny that there was not a lot left to save in the house and that she would need to replace almost everything. A tear ran down her face, and she wondered what she would do.

Chris hugged Destiny and said that things would take some time. "In the meantime, you and Holly can stay at the B and B as long as you need to. Let's head back to the B and B and see the girls. That will cheer you up. There's nothing we can do right now."

When Destiny and Chris got back to the B and B, Amber, Eric, and the girls were there.

"Chris, can you play with the girls? I need to talk to your parents. I'll see you in a few minutes," Destiny said.

Destiny told his parents what was happening with the house. "I have lost almost everything. I have received money for the repair of my house. I would like to pay you something for your kindness in letting Holly and I stay here," Destiny said.

"Don't you even dare think about paying anything. We love having you both here. You're a joy to have, and you bring so much fun to our inn," Amber said.

"There is something that brought you here, and it's called fate. Let's just see how it plays out and see where life takes you," Eric said. Destiny hugged both Chris's parents and thanked them for their kindness.

Destiny, Amber, and Eric heard the girls giggling and having a great time, so the three went to investigate. They were all dancing.

Destiny said, laughing, "I think I'll join you."

It was a lovely evening, but as the time was running late, Sapphire and Holly needed to get some sleep. So Destiny brought Holly to her room and put her pajamas on. Sapphire rested in bed until her dad came to get her.

Chapter 6

Daniel went to visit Paige in the morning. After he and Paige talked about Chris, he realized how wrong he was to have treated Chris so badly. Daniel drove home from Paige's house and asked Chris if he could talk to him. Daniel walked up to Chris, sat, and began to talk to him.

He said, "I just left Paige's house, and she made me realize what a good man you are, especially a great dad. You always put your daughter first before your own needs. I can see the love Sapphire has for you and that she is very happy. I'm so sorry for my behavior lately. The reason I stayed away from home for so long was so that I wouldn't fight with you. I know that I have competed with you our whole lives, but I felt I could never live up to your standards. So I fought with you and hurt you. It's time that I stand on my own two feet and live my life to the fullest. I like Paige, and if she is a part of your daughter's life and yours, then I need to be more respectful. I am going to try and be a better brother, but my antics will probably won't go away totally. After all, we are still brothers."

Chris laughed. "Yes, we are." He shook Daniel's hand. "I am so happy that you and I can be friends. I am sorry for anything that I have done to make you feel this way. I will try to be aware of my behavior and actions too."

This time the brothers embraced.

"You're an awesome brother, Daniel," Chris said.

"You're okay too, brother," Daniel said with a smile. Just as the two stood there in the living room, Destiny walked in and asked if everything was all right.

"Everything is good," Chris said.

"Sapphire is in our bedroom, waiting for you," Destiny said.

"I guess it's getting late. I'll go and get her," Chris said, but when he opened the door, Sapphire was fast asleep. "I'll go and warm up the truck." Chris then bundled Sapphire up and carried her to the truck. "I'll see you tomorrow, Destiny. Sweet dreams, my dear," Chris said as he kissed her on the cheek.

"Good night," Destiny said as she kissed Sapphire on the forehead. "I'll see you tomorrow."

Once Chris left, Daniel told Destiny that he and his brother had bonded and were going to try to work through their issues. "It feels good to have my brother back into my life. Oh, and I'm sorry that I was such a jerk when I first met you," Daniel said.

"I knew things would work out for the two of you. Brothers have stronger bonds than you think," Destiny said.

"I know that this will make my parents happier too," Daniel said.

"Well, it's getting late, so I'm off to bed. Good night, Daniel," Destiny said.

"Good night, Destiny," Daniel said.

When Chris got home, he put Sapphire to bed and then went directly to his bedroom. He tried to get a few hours of sleep before going to work, but when morning arrived, Sapphire went into Chris's room and jumped on the bed.

"Good morning, Daddy!"

"Oh, you little monkey!" Chris said to Sapphire as he grabbed her and tickled her.

"What's for breakfast? I'm hungry!" Sapphire announced as she watched her daddy get up.

"Let's go check in the refrigerator," Chris said as he held Sapphire's hand and headed into the kitchen.

Chris took the Christmas hat off the hook and started to sing a breakfast song. Sapphire just laughed and laughed at her silly daddy.

"We have Christmas pancakes, Rudolph's scrambled eggs, or Frosty cereal," Chris said.

"I think that I'll have some Christmas pancakes with milk, please," Sapphire announced. "Can I have some blueberries too?" she asked.

"Sure," Chris replied. "When you finish your pancakes, you'll need to get dressed and ready for school," Chris said.

"Do I have to? I want to stay home with you," Sapphire said.

"You have to go to school so you can see your friends," Chris said.

"I wish Holly could go to my school," Sapphire said.

"She is homeschooled, sweetie," Chris told her.

"I miss Holly," Sapphire said, looking sad.

"I'll tell you what, you go to school, and I'll call Destiny and ask her if she and Holly would like to come for supper tonight," Chris said.

"Yay! I hope they come!"

"Me too. Now go and get ready for school."

"Okay," she replied.

Once Sapphire left for school, Chris got ready for work. Before leaving, he called Destiny and invited her to dinner. She replied that she and Holly would be happy to come over for dinner. Destiny said, "It's hard to keep these two apart."

"Well, I'd like to say I don't want to be apart from you and Holly either," Chris said over the phone.

"I feel that way too," Destiny replied. "Hey, I want to thank you for your letter. It was beautiful, and it warmed my heart knowing that you care for me and want to see where our journey takes us. This makes me so happy."

"I think we make a good team, not only for us but for the girls too," Chris said.

"I think so too," Destiny replied.

"It was great to talk to you this morning, but I need to go to work," Chris said.

"I need to get Holly ready too so I can get to work too," Destiny said.

"I'll see you tonight at six o'clock," Chris told her.

Chris worked very hard to do all his work and leave early. He finished his day and headed home to make supper and tidy up a bit.

Chris wasn't too worried about the house because Paige helped keep the house clean for him. Chris was so appreciative of her kindness. When Chris walked in, Paige announced she had another date with Daniel and they were going night skiing. Paige was very excited and said her goodbyes to Chris and Sapphire.

"Have a good time!" Chris said.

"Does Uncle Daniel like Paige?" Sapphire asked.

"It appears so," Chris said.

"So what are we having for supper?" Sapphire asked.

"Pasta and Swedish meatballs," he replied.

"Why don't you get some lettuce, tomatoes, and cucumbers and we'll make a salad too?" Chris asked.

"I can't wait till Holly gets here!" Sapphire said, jumping.

"She'll be here before you know it," Chris said.

Destiny and Holly drove up the driveway. Holly rang the doorbell, and Sapphire ran to the door and let them in.

"Good evening!" Destiny said.

"It's nice to see you again," Chris said with a kiss to Destiny's cheek.

"I hope everyone's hungry because there is a ton of food," Sapphire announced.

"You have a lovely home. I love your Christmas decorations inside and outside too. You did a great job," Destiny said to Chris.

Everyone sat and began to enjoy their supper while having a great time sharing stories, telling jokes, and laughing. Once supper was over, the two girls went into Sapphire's room to play. Destiny helped Chris with the dishes while talking about Holly. Just as they were finishing the dishes, a song came over the radio, and they began to dance. This brought them so much joy.

"Thank you for this dance, my dear," Chris said as he kissed her soft hand.

"You are welcome, my prince," Destiny said. "Not to bring this moment crashing down, but I need to talk about Holly. You know," Destiny continued, "Holly has been a little sad that she lost a lot of her things in the fire. Christmas is coming, and I'm sure that she will get some wonderful things. I know that my mom will send her a gift, and I could buy a few things that she lost that were under the Christmas tree. It is only a few weeks away. It's just that money is so tight. It's going to take most of the insurance money to rebuild my home, and I'm trying to save money to buy new furniture, curtains, rugs, lamps, and chairs."

Chris held Destiny's face in his hands and sweetly told her that everything would be all right. "Good things will come from this. You will see," Chris told her.

"I just have to take one day at a time," Destiny said.

After talking with Destiny, the phone rang. Chris got a call saying that two of his workers were sick and wouldn't be at work tomorrow.

"Feel better, guys," Chris told him and hung up. "This is not good news with the holiday upon us and the busiest time of the year," Chris said.

"Why don't I come and help you for the day? I can catch up on my work later," Destiny suggested.

"You would do that for me?" Chris asked. "That would be great!" Chris said with a big hug. "I'll ask Paige if she could watch Holly too," Chris said.

"Okay, great," Destiny said.

Just as they were finishing up their conversation, the girls came out.

"Let's play a game," Sapphire asked.

"What do you want to play?" Destiny asked.

"Let's play a guessing game," Sapphire said. "It can be about any topic, and we have to say what we think the answer would be."

"That sounds like fun," Destiny said. They played the game until it got late.

Chris noticed the time. "It's been a fun evening, but it's time for me to get Holly to bed," Destiny said.

"I had such a wonderful evening," Chris said.

"Me too," Destiny said.

"Daddy, can Holly sleep over? Please! I have an extra sleeping bag."

"If Destiny says it's all right," Chris said. "You know, it's not such a bad idea to have you sleep over too," Chris said to Destiny. "We can get an early start on the farm. I'll sleep on the couch, and you can have my bed."

"That's very kind of you, Chris," Destiny said.

"Yay!" The girls jumped for joy as they ran to Sapphire's room to get ready for bed.

"Are you sure? I can sleep on the couch." Destiny asked.

"Young ladies sleep in beds and not on the couch," he said with a smile. Destiny and Chris stayed up talking till midnight and then headed to bed.

"I'll see you in the morning, Chris," Destiny said.

"Good night, sweetheart," Chris said.

When morning came, Chris was up making breakfast. "Bacon, eggs, and toast!" Chris yelled. "Is anyone hungry?" Sapphire and Holly came out of their bedroom wiping their eyes. Destiny followed the girls.

"Good morning, Chris," Destiny said. Destiny ran up to the girls and gave them one big hug and then tickled their tummies. The girls giggled and then sat at the table. "Everything looks great, Chris," Destiny said.

"Well, let's eat up. It's going to be a busy day," Chris announced.

After breakfast, Destiny went to get the girls and herself dressed for the day. Luckily, Destiny always carried extra clothes in the car.

Chapter 7

Paige came into Chris's house with a big smile.

"Good morning, Paige!" Chris said. "It looks like you had a wonderful evening skiing yesterday."

"Yes, I did," she responded, still smiling. "Daniel is a true gentleman and is very kind to me."

"I am happy for you and Daniel," Chris said. "Would you mind watching Holly today too?"

"I would be happy to. We're the three musketeers," Paige said. "Today is going to be a lot of fun, girls."

"What are we doing today?" Sapphire asked.

"I thought that we could bring Dakota for a walk and then go sledding," Paige said.

"That sounds good." The girls held hands, dancing around the table.

"Daddy, when can we go and see Santa Claus?" Sapphire asked.

"How about after you and Holly go to the shelter to read to the dogs on Saturday? I'd like to bring the girls to the shelter, or we could go together, Destiny," Chris suggested.

"I like the idea of all of us going together," Destiny voiced.

"Then Saturday it is!" Chris said.

"Yay!" Sapphire and Holly said, jumping.

"Right now, Destiny and I need to get to work, so we will see you girls later," Chris said with a kiss to each girl's cheek.

"I'm ready, Chris!" Destiny said as she went to the girls to give them a hug and kiss.

"Thanks, Paige. We'll see you later."

"You're welcome, and have a nice day," Paige voiced to Chris and Destiny.

"Let's play with Dakota," Holly said to Sapphire.

"We can read a story to Dakota," Sapphire said. "I think that she would like that."

Chris and Destiny headed out for a mile down the road and came across several beautiful trees ready to be cut down.

"I hope you brought your muscles with you," Chris said, teasing Destiny.

"Don't you worry about me. I'm strong as a horse," Destiny said with a smile. Chris got the chain saw out of his truck and began cutting the trees down. He wrapped each tree as Destiny loaded the truck.

"I guess you are pretty strong," he said as Destiny tossed the trees into the truck bed.

"No messing around with me," she said jokingly. "Chris, do people ever want a live tree that they can use for Christmas and then plant the tree in the spring?" Destiny asked.

"They sure do," Chris told her. "I already have several in the tree lot. When people buy a planted tree, I give them a free box of ornaments. I think that it's a great idea to promote replanting of trees. It's good for the environment.

"Time is sure flying by fast. Look, it's already noontime. Let's stop and eat," Chris suggested.

Chris laid down a thick blanket on the ground and brought out a picnic basket filled with chicken sandwiches, grapes, vegetable sticks, some brownies for dessert, and a thermos filled with hot apple cider. They both sat on the blanket and enjoyed their meal.

"Destiny, I've been thinking about Christmas, and I really need to know what to get Holly," Chris said.

"She used to have a collection of snow globes, but she lost them in the fire. It broke her heart."

"I have a great idea! I'll get her an awesome Christmas snow globe," Chris said.

"Okay, Chris. What about an idea for Sapphire's gift?" Destiny asked.

"She loves everything about wildlife, so anything in that area would be great. As for you, my dear, you will have to wait and see what I get you," Chris said teasingly.

"I think I have something nice in store for you too," Destiny said. "I can't believe Christmas is coming up so soon," Destiny went on to say. "I love the holidays. It's the time of the year when people are kinder, more generous, and more forgiving. It's a time of peace and joy."

"I agree. It's a wonderful time of the year," Chris said. "Do you think you'll get to see your mother this Christmas?"

"I'm hoping to see my mom. She is supposed to call me this week and let me know what she's doing for Christmas. I'm hoping that she'll stay for a bit. I miss her so," Destiny told Chris.

"What's her name?" he asked.

"Virginia Wright," she replied. "She's an amazing woman. I can't wait for you to meet her."

"I look forward to meeting her," Chris said with a smile.

Once lunch was over, Chris and Destiny went back to work, cutting down trees and loading them onto the truck. A few hours later, they decided to pack up and go home early to see the girls. When they got home, they unloaded the truck to the Christmas tree lot and headed into the house. When Chris and Destiny walked into the house, they saw Sapphire lying on the couch, covered with a blanket. Holly was on the floor, playing next to her.

"What happened?" Chris asked Paige.

Paige responded, saying, "Sapphire was sledding down the hill and fell off the sled, sliding into a bank of snow. Dakota went running after her when the snow loosened and fell on top of her. She was scared but all right. Holly and I ran over to her and wiped the snow off of her. She was very cold, so we brought her back home. I made her some hot chocolate, and now she's resting."

Chris gave Sapphire a big hug. "I'm glad that you're all right."

"Me too!" Destiny said, rubbing her forehead.

"Thanks, Paige, for taking care of her," Chris said.

"Of course, she's my buddy," Paige responded.

"Well, I think that we should call it a night and let Sapphire get some rest," Chris said.

"I agree, Chris, and we will see you tomorrow morning," Destiny voiced.

"I'll pick you and Holly up in the morning to go to the shelter."

"See you tomorrow then," Destiny said.

"Are you feeling better, Sapphire?" Chris asked.

"Yes, but I'm just tired," Sapphire replied.

"Why don't I make you some chicken noodle soup? We can watch a Christmas movie, and you can rest with me on the couch," Chris asked.

"Okay, Daddy," Sapphire said.

So Chris and Sapphire enjoyed their evening together and went to bed early. When Destiny got home, Amber said that her mother had called and asked for a call back.

"Hi, Mom, just calling you back," Destiny said.

"I'm sorry about your house, sweetheart. How are things going?" her mother said.

"I'm just taking it one day at a time. The construction crew is starting this week. I'm pretty happy about that."

"Were you able to save anything?" Virginia asked.

"Some of our clothes, a couple of Holly's book, and a picture of me and Holly on my bedroom nightstand. My table, stove, refrigerator, and cabinets are all right. They just need a deep cleaning. But as for the rest of my things, they have too much smoke damage. My family photo albums were burned up and many of Holly's toys. This saddens me very much," Destiny told her mother.

"Things will work out fine. You'll see. If you would like, I'll be flying out in a few days to see you. I have a very big surprise for you."

"What is it?" Destiny asked.

"You'll find out when I get there."

"I have a sleeper bed that you can use in my room," Destiny said.

"That's great! It'll be nice just to be with you and Holly. I miss you both so much!" Virginia said. "Is there anything that I can bring you?"

"Yes. You know the small dolls you bought for Holly when she visits you? Could you bring them so she'll have something to play with?" Destiny asked.

"I'd be happy to," Virginia replied. "I may have a few more surprises for Holly too."

"Thanks, Mom. You're the best!" Destiny said. "I'll see you soon, Mom. I love you!" Destiny said. "Oh, Mom, I forgot to tell you that the day you come here is the mistletoe dance. Be sure to bring some extra warm clothes. It's cold in Alaska."

"I'll see you in a few days. Take care, sweetheart, and give Holly my love," Virginia voiced.

"I will. Bye, Mom."

When she got off the phone, she asked Amber if there was anything else that needed to be done for the mistletoe dance.

"You can help me pack some things up, but I have everything pretty well as set, but the day of the dance, I'll need you to decorate those ten themed trees and set up some decorations for the tables."

"I'd be happy to," Destiny said.

"I can't believe that it's coming up so fast. I'm very excited!" Amber voiced.

"It will be fun," Destiny said.

"I noticed that you have some children's book in the lobby. May I bring one to our room and read it to Holly?"

"Of course, that's why they are there," Amber said.

Destiny picked out a book for Holly and went into their room and got ready for bed.

"You have a busy day tomorrow with the shelter and then going to see Santa," Destiny told Holly.

Destiny brought Holly to bed and then sat on her bed, reading a story. Destiny lay down and cuddled with Holly till she fell asleep. Then having a book to read, she sat on her bed. When she opened the book, the letter Chris wrote fell out. She read the letter and felt blessed to have such a kind, gentle man in her life. She thought that she was beginning to fall hard for him. She felt Chris treated her with so much respect it made her like him even more. She thought that she'd talk to her mom about it when she arrived. Destiny laid the letter down and fell fast asleep.

"Good morning, Mom!" Holly said. "We've got a busy day!"

"Good morning, my sweet girl!" Destiny replied.

"Let's get up and have breakfast," Holly said.

Eric, Amber, and Daniel were already awake in the kitchen, enjoying their breakfast along with their visitors.

"Good morning, everyone," Destiny said.

"How are you two ladies doing this lovely morning?" Amber asked as she went up to Holly and hugged her.

"We're good," Destiny said.

"Today we're going to the shelter with Chris and Sapphire and then to see Santa," Holly told everyone.

"Wow, you do have a busy day," Daniel said with a smile.

"Let's eat quick and get dressed," Holly voiced.

"We have plenty of time to eat and get ready," Destiny told Holly.

Just as Destiny and Holly were finishing their breakfast, Chris and Sapphire came in.

"Everyone ready?" Sapphire asked excitedly.

"We just have to get dressed, and we'll be right out," Destiny said.

"Hurry, Mom, let's get dressed," Holly said.

While they were getting dressed, it gave Chris a chance to talk to his family. Sapphire ran up to Grandma, Grandpa, and Daniel and gave them all hugs.

"It's nice to see everyone," Chris said. "How's the mistletoe dance coming along?" Chris whispered.

"Your father and I are getting the tables situated, and Daniel is going to set up the dance floor. Today we're going to do a lot of the decorating. If you could set up the ten trees tomorrow, it would be very helpful," Amber said.

"I'll do that after work tomorrow," Chris said.

"Could you have Destiny meet you there with the supplies to decorate all the trees?" Amber asked.

"I'm sure she will. I'll talk to her later about it," Chris replied.

"Okay, we're ready," Holly said, coming out of the room.

"Let's go read to some dogs," Chris said as the four of them jumped into the truck and headed to the shelter.

When they got there, Destiny gave more of her homemade blankets to the dogs. They all got some books to read to the dogs. There were lots of dogs with several other people reading to them.

"This is a great program," Chris said.

"I really enjoy it too," Destiny said.

An hour later, everyone gathered their books and put them back on the rack.

"I hope more of them get adopted," Holly said to the woman in charge.

"I hope so too."

Once they finished reading, the owner wished the girls a good day. "See you girls later. Thank you for coming," she replied.

"So, girls, are you ready to go see Santa?" Chris asked.

"Let's go, Daddy!" Sapphire said excitedly as she grabbed his hand, hurrying to the truck.

"Come on, Mommy, catch up," Holly said with a giggle.

"I'm coming! I'm coming!" Destiny shouted.

The four of them got into the truck and headed to the mall. "I'm so excited to see Santa!" Sapphire said.

"What are you going to ask him for?" Chris asked.

"I can't tell you. It may not come true," Sapphire replied.

"How about you, Holly? Do you know what you want?" Chris asked.

"I lost a lot of my things, but what would make me happy is—"

"Don't tell, Holly. Only Santa gets to know what you want for Christmas," Sapphire interrupted.

"Well, whatever it is, I'm sure Santa will make your wishes come true," Destiny said.

"We're here! We're here!" Sapphire yelled as she unbuckled her seat belt.

They all got out of the truck, walking hand in hand together into the mall. It surely was beginning to feel like they were becoming a family. Chris and Destiny looked at each other and then at the girls and smiled.

"This is great!" Chris announced.

This feels so right, Destiny thought.

When they saw Santa in his jolly red suit, white beard, and blue eyes, they got very excited hearing his ho ho hos!

As Santa was talking to the other children, the girls got a little antsy and couldn't wait to talk to him. They got in line behind some other children. Mrs. Claus was there in her beautiful red Christmas dress, and a few of Santa's elves were helping out. When it was finally their turn, Sapphire went first.

"Hi, Santa, how are you?" she asked.

"Ho ho ho! Aren't you the sweet little girl to ask me that? I'm doing well. What's your name?" Santa asked.

"My name is Sapphire," she replied.

"Well, that's a pretty name," Santa said.

"So tell Santa, what would you like for Christmas?"

"I have two wishes. I have so many toys at my house that my wish is for my best friend, Holly. Her house caught on fire, and she lost her toys. You can give her my toy."

"You are a very sweet girl, Sapphire. I will certainly give her a toy, but I will leave something special for you," Santa said.

"Thanks, Santa. My second wish is for my daddy. I want my daddy to marry Destiny. She's so nice, and her daughter is my best friend. I would like to have a mommy."

"Now that's a tall order. We will have to see about that," Santa said.

"Thanks again, Santa," Sapphire said as she hugged him.

"You're very welcome," Santa replied.

"Hello, my dear," Mrs. Claus said, talking to Sapphire. "Would you like a candy cane?"

"I would love one. Thank you," Sapphire said. "Merry Christmas!" Sapphire said as she walked down the steps. Sapphire then took Holly by the hand and walked back up to Santa and introduced her. "Santa, this is my friend Holly."

"Hello, Holly, it's a pleasure to meet you," Santa said. Sapphire walked down the steps to her dad.

"Would you like to sit on my lap and tell Santa what you would like for Christmas?"

"Sure." Holly climbed on his lap and told Santa about all her toys she lost.

"I'm so sorry to hear this," Santa said. "Well, I want to make you very happy this Christmas, so can you tell me what you would like?"

"I'd like to live back in my home with my mommy," Holly said. "I would also like if my mommy would settle down with Chris. He's a nice man, and he's fun."

"That's a tall order," Santa said. "I will see what I can do for you."

"I wanted to tell you that right now, my mommy and me are living at Adams's Bed and Breakfast. The owners, Amber and Eric, are very nice, but I miss my house."

"Things will be all right, Holly," Santa said. "I'll bring you a very special gift just from Santa. You have a Merry Christmas, Holly," Santa said as he helped her down off his lap. An elf helped Holly down the stairs where Mrs. Claus was waiting to greet her.

"Holly," Mrs. Claus said, "I'm so happy to meet you. How about a candy cane?" she asked.

"I would like one very much," Holly told her. Mrs. Claus handed her a candy cane and guided her to her mom standing by the bottom of the steps.

"How cool was that, girls!" Destiny said.

"Santa is a very kind old man," Sapphire said. "I hope he makes my wishes come true. And yours too, Holly."

"I like Mrs. Claus too," Holly said. "I know Santa will make my wishes come true. He's Santa."

"Now that we've seen Santa, I need to get back to the tree lot and help the staff with the trees," Chris announced.

"We can all help," Destiny said.

"I'm sure Sapphire and Holly can pass out some cocoa and cookies to the customers," Chris said.

"I can also help out making some wreaths for you," Destiny said.

"Thanks! That's great, Destiny!"

Back at the tree lot, Chris saw how busy the tree lot was as many people were buying their Christmas tree.

"Okay, people, let's get out there and sell some trees," Chris said to Destiny, Sapphire, and Holly.

The staff was happy to see Chris and the girls pitch in. One customer came up to Chris and asked him if he could carve him a cardinal.

"It's for my wife. She loves cardinals," the gentleman said.

"Of course. When do you need it?" Chris asked.

"When you get it done, hopefully before Christmas. Just call me when it's done, and I'll come pick it up."

"I'll start the cardinal after we close the Christmas lot," Chris said.

Now Destiny was very excited because she would get to see Chris carve something and that was her favorite bird too.

"This is really fun," Destiny said to Chris. Destiny really loved the scent of the trees and giving personal attention to the customers. "I can see why you love your tree farm so much, Chris," Destiny said.

Destiny helped Chris by decorating the Christmas wreaths. Sapphire and Holly were passing out some cookies and hot chocolate. It was a good night. Once the Christmas tree lot closed, Chris had the girls go into the house to warm up. Chris asked Destiny if she would like to see him using his chain saw to create a cardinal. Chris would also be using his ax, mallet, and chisel. Destiny was so excited. While Chris was beginning his carving, Destiny sat and watched him. It was amazing to see such precise cutting, a piece of wood carved off here and there and lots of sawdust going back and forth on the wood just to get the exact shape. It was beginning to take the form of a bird.

"I love it!" Destiny said.

"Thanks!" he replied. A few hours went by before Chris finished his carving. "Now all I have to do is paint the cardinal red," Chris said to Destiny.

Chris went to the garage shelf and took the paint down and began painting the cardinal. Just as he was putting the final touches on the bird, Sapphire and Holly came back out.

"Daddy, it's beautiful!" Sapphire said.

"I love it!" Holly said. "It's my mom's favorite bird."

"You're a very talented young man," Destiny said.

"I'll call the gentleman tomorrow. He will be very happy, and his wife will be so surprised," Chris said. "I'm tired," Chris said. "It's time to turn in. I'll see you lovely ladies tomorrow," Chris said to Destiny and Holly.

"I'm pretty tired too, Mommy," Holly said.

"Then let's get you home to bed," Destiny said.

"Good night, Chris and Sapphire. I'll see you tomorrow," Destiny said.

Once Chris got Sapphire to bed, he brought Dakota out to run around outside. Chris enjoyed watching her as she pushed her nose into the snow and then rolled around in it. It was so cute.

The next morning, Destiny came out of the bedroom and saw Amber and Eric packing some supplies up.

"What's going on?" Destiny asked.

"We are making the final touches for the mistletoe dance," Amber said. "Will I see you later, Destiny? The Christmas trees are waiting." Amber winked.

"Sure. I'll be down after breakfast. I'll get Holly dressed, and then I'll head over. While eating breakfast with Holly, Destiny remembered that her mom was coming to the bed-and-breakfast.

"I can't wait till Grandma arrives," Holly stated.

"Neither can I," Destiny replied.

After breakfast, Sapphire brought Dakota outside for a while. Then Chris came out, and they brought the dog out for a walk.

"This is such a nice day, Daddy," Sapphire said.

"It sure is," Chris said.

When they came back from their walk, they gathered their things and headed to the barn to set up the trees. Once finished, he called Destiny to let her know that he and Sapphire were in the barn.

Destiny and Holly collected all the donated supplies for the trees and headed over to the barn to get started. Chris had already set up the ten Christmas trees, and so they were ready for decorating. Holly and Sapphire handed Destiny the ornaments used for each themed tree.

"Hi, Destiny. I'm so glad to see you," Amber said. "I can't wait to see your themed trees."

The first tree decorated was the Poinsettias Christmas. It was beautifully covered in red silk poinsettias, stars, white ornaments, gold ribbons, and a gold star for the top.

The Angels Watching over Us tree was filled with angels, harps, feathers, horns, stars, gold garlands, and an angel on the top of the tree.

The Seed of Hope tree was filled with plant, fruit, birdseed, and vegetable seed packages; gloves; a small planter; a watering can; and a bird for the top.

The Vintage Christmas tree was filled with beautiful vintage ornaments and laces.

The 12 Days of Christmas tree was filled with a partridge, two turtledoves, three French hens, four calling birds, and the rest of the items from the song.

The Comfort and Joy tree was filled with a variety of teas, teacups, relaxing books, lotion, and a fan.

The Woodland Wonders tree was filled with small furry animals, pine cones, birdseed balls, and hollies.

The Gingerbread tree was filled with gingerbread cookies placed in baggies and tied with red bows that Amber and Sapphire made, red-and-gold ornaments, garlands, and a large gingerbread man cookie for the top.

The Caring tree was for people at the homeless shelter. Anyone at the gathering could bring in items, such as scarves, mittens, gloves, socks, and hats, that would be gathered together and brought to the shelter.

Lastly, the Children's Craft tree had a few color ornaments, but since it was meant to be decorated by the children's homemade ornaments from the craft table, Destiny only used a few of hers and a star.

"All of this decorating is certainly fun, but I'm exhausted," Amber said.

"Now that I'm finished with the trees," Destiny said to Amber, "why don't you and Eric come out with Holly and me for lunch?" Destiny said, "It's the least that I could do for you two."

"Sounds lovely. We'd be happy to go," Amber said with a smile.

The four of them got into two separate cars and met at the diner downtown. They all ordered their food.

"I'm so glad you came. I wanted to thank you for being so kind to me and Holly. It means so much to us. I don't know how I could ever pay it back," Destiny told Amber and Eric.

"As I told you before, you were meant to be here. It's fate," Amber said. "You and Holly are two very special people. You have raised a beautiful daughter on your own, and that is no easy task. Eric and I have grown quite fond of you two. I have noticed that Chris and Sapphire have grown quite close to you both too."

"I have a lot of fun with Sapphire and Chris," Holly said. "Sapphire is my best friend."

"You and Sapphire bring so much joy into our lives. It's nice to have little ones around," Amber said.

"I agree. You two are very special to us," Eric said.

"Well, here comes our food. Let's eat up!" Eric said.

The luncheon was wonderful, and everyone enjoyed themselves. Just as they were getting ready to leave, Destiny's mother called.

"Hi, Mom! Where are you?" Destiny said.

"I just landed at the Whispering Pines airport," Virginia told Destiny. "Could you come and pick me up?"

"Sure. I can't wait to see you!" Destiny said.

"Me too," her mother said.

"I'm just leaving the diner now. See you in a few," Destiny said. Destiny paid for the lunch and headed out to the airport.

"Thank you for the lunch. It was lovely," Amber said. "I'm looking forward to meeting your mother."

"See you at the bed-and-breakfast," Eric said.

Destiny and Holly got into the car and headed to the airport. It was only a few miles away.

"I can't wait to see Grandma," Holly voiced.

"It's been a while since we saw her," Destiny said. "I can't wait either."

Destiny arrived at the airport and saw her mom coming toward them. A tear ran down her cheek.

Holly saw her and yelled, "Grandma! Grandma!"

When she got to the car, Holly jumped out of the car and hugged her.

"Look at how big you have gotten, Holly!" Virginia said excitedly.

"I'm a big girl now. I'm five," Holly said.

"How was your flight from Utah?" Destiny asked.

"It was wonderful," Virginia said.

"We are heading to the Adams's Bed and Breakfast. You're going to love Amber and Eric. They're such nice people," Destiny told her mother.

"I'm sure that I will," Virginia said. "When do I get to meet Chris?"

"Probably after work. I'll call and leave him a message," Destiny told her.

"I have a surprise for you two when we get to the bed-and-breakfast," Virginia told them.

Chapter 8

When Destiny, Holly, and Virginia got to the B and B, Amber and Eric welcomed her inside.

"It's so nice to meet you," Amber said. "A visitor just left, so there is a vacancy if you want the room. It's right next to Destiny's room."

"Sounds great! Thank you," Virginia said.

Eric asked, "May I take your bags? You certainly have a lot of them."

"I brought some extra things for my girls," Virginia responded. "I have a few surprises for Destiny and Holly. Let me unpack, and then we can all talk," Virginia said.

Once Virginia unpacked her bags, she came out of her room with the few gifts. First, she gave Amber and Eric a gift. "I just wanted to show you my appreciation for taking in my daughter and granddaughter," Virginia said with a smile. She passed them a beautiful tin lantern with a holiday candle.

"This was so kind of you, Virginia," Amber said. "I love it!" Amber said. "Look at all these details."

"It's very nice," Eric said. "Thank you."

"You're welcome," Virginia responded. "Destiny, Holly, come sit next to me," Virginia said. "Now, Holly, I know how upset you are about losing your toys, so I thought this may make you feel a little better," Virginia said.

"Thanks, Grandma," Holly said as she took the present from her grandmother. Holly unwrapped the gifts, and inside were a few new books and a beautiful fairy doll with a pink costume, blond hair, blue eyes, fairy wings, and a glittery mask. "I love the presents!" Holly said excitedly as they were all sitting together. Then she gave her grandma a hug. "Thank you so much!"

"I'm so glad," Virginia said with a smile. "I also brought a few other toys that you had at my house."

"Thank you so much!" Holly said.

"Destiny, I have something very special for you." As Destiny opened her gift, she looked down in the bag and saw two scrapbooks.

"These pictures are of you over the years—from infancy, as a young child, teenager, and young adult. There were also pictures from Holly's birth to the present," Virginia said.

"I can't believe you did this! How?" Destiny said with tears in her eyes.

"Most of the photographs that you lost in the fire have been replaced. I called all the family and my friends to see if they had any photographs that they could copy and send to me. I got hundreds of pictures of you growing up and of Holly. A few weeks ago, many family members and my friends got together at my house and made you these two scrapbooks for you."

"I am so touched by this. You're the best mother!" Destiny said. "Be sure to thank them all for me."

"I'm glad that you like it," Virginia said.

Holly sat next to her mother and looked at all the photographs in the scrapbook.

"I can't wait to show Chris," Destiny said. "Speaking of Chris, he just pulled into the driveway," Destiny said.

"How nice. I have been very eager to meet this young man," Virginia said.

Chris and Sapphire walked into the house, where they were warmly greeted by his parents and introduced to Virginia.

"Hello, Mrs. Wright. It's so nice to meet you," Chris said with a handshake. "This is my daughter, Sapphire."

"Nice to meet you both," Virginia said. "Now, Chris, we have to straighten out this Mrs. Wright thing. You must call me Virginia, and we give hugs in our family. As for you, sweet Sapphire, you can call me

Ms. Virginia. I have heard a lot about you, Chris," Virginia said. "My daughter seems to like you quite a bit. I can see why."

Everyone laughed.

"We have another son. You'll meet him at the mistletoe dance this evening," Amber said.

"I look forward to meeting him," Virginia said. "This dance sounds like it will be a lot of fun!"

"It's going to be great!" Amber said. "The mistletoe dance starts in an hour, so we should probably get ready," Amber said to everyone. "Everything is set at the barn, and we're rearing to go."

Destiny and Chris drove down to the barn with Virginia and the girls. Chris opened the car door for Virginia and helped her out of the car. Then Chris opened the door for Destiny and took her hand. The girls ran ahead.

"It looks beautiful!" Virginia said. "Destiny, did you do all the decorating?"

"Just the trees and the tables," she said.

"I thought so," Virginia replied. "There's so much to see. It's lovely."

Amber, Eric, and Daniel all showed up at the dance. Paige was also on her way to the dance.

"The community did an amazing job," Amber said.

"Yes, they sure did," Eric said.

The community was arriving by the dozens.

"Before we begin the dance, I'd like to introduce Daniel to Virginia," Amber said. Amber walked up to Virginia, and she introduced her son Daniel to her.

"Virginia, this is my son Daniel," Amber said.

"It's nice to meet you," Virginia responded.

Suddenly, Paige arrived and walked over to Daniel.

"Virginia," Chris said, "this is Sapphire's babysitter, Paige. She's a sweetheart, and she's great with her, and I don't know what I would do without her."

"It's very nice to meet you, Paige," Virginia said.

"Paige!" Sapphire said, running to her and giving her a big hug. Then Holly followed suit.

"I agree. Paige is very special," Daniel said, taking her hand in his.

"It's so nice to have everyone here," Amber said.

"Now that everyone is here, let's get the party started," Amber said as she walked up onto the stage to make an announcement.

"Hello, everyone, and thank you so much for coming to the mistletoe dance event. I also want to thank everyone for helping make this dance possible. Now as all of you know, this charity event is to help someone very special among us. We have kept this a surprise, and amazingly enough, she hadn't figured it out. Destiny and Holly, will you both come up here?" Amber said.

Destiny was in shock as she walked up to the stage.

"Now before you say anything, I'd like to tell you that this mistletoe dance is for you and Holly to help you get back on your feet. Everyone here has pitched in to make this evening one you'll never forget."

"I was helping you with the trees and table decorations, and I would never have guessed that you were doing this for us," Destiny expressed. Destiny was in tears and so surprised. Destiny walked up to the microphone and said, "There are no words in my heart that could express the gratitude that all of you have displayed for my daughter and I. It has been very difficult for us, but we have been taking one day at a time. Now I believe that everything will be all right. Thank you so much! I also want to thank Amber and Eric for opening their house to us. It has meant so much to us."

Everyone cheered. Amber hugged Destiny and Holly, and then Eric helped them down the steps. Holly stood next to her mom with tears in her eyes when she realized what the dance was all about. Destiny was so happy and thanked everyone again.

As Destiny and Holly came down the stairs of the stage, people were waiting to meet them. Chris and Sapphire were there to hug them as the crowd waited to meet her.

"This is so overwhelming!" Destiny said.

Once things calmed down, Amber took the microphone again and announced, "We have a lot of events happening tonight, so let's all enjoy the evening." Again, everyone cheered.

"So what do you want to do first?" Chris asked the girls.

"I want to go and have our faces painted," Sapphire announced. She took Holly by the hand and said, "Let's go and get our faces painted."

Destiny and Chris followed behind the girls. The girls had to wait their turn. A few minutes later, it was the girls' turn. Sapphire and Holly sat in their chairs and let the two artists paint their faces. Holly had a fairy design on her face, and Sapphire had a peacock face. They were so excited when they saw their faces in the mirror.

"Your faces look beautiful," Destiny voiced.

"They sure do," Chris said.

"So what do you girls want to do now?"

"We want to go and make an ornament for the Children's Craft tree," Sapphire said.

"Yay! Let's go, Sapphire!" Holly voiced excitedly.

"We're right behind you, girls," Destiny said. As the girls sat to design their craft, Chris told the girls that they would be right back.

"We're going to the dance floor," Chris said. "You girls stay here till we come back."

"Okay," Sapphire said, "we will," Holly voiced as the two girls were busy making their crafts.

Chris took Destiny's hand as the country band began to play their music and led her to the dance floor. As they danced, Destiny was still in shock and telling Chris just how happy she was that so many people cared about her and Holly.

"You are pretty special, and I did tell you that things would work out," Chris said.

"Yes, you did," Destiny said with a smile.

As they danced to the music, Chris asked if Destiny would like to have this song as their song.

"It's a beautiful song. I would like that," she replied.

"This feels so right to be dancing with you. I can feel my heart beating so fast just having you this close to me," Chris said.

"I love the way it feels when you're this close to me too. You mean the world to me, and with each passing day, I feel closer and closer to you," Destiny said. As the song ended, they gave each other a kiss.

"That was nice," Chris said. Destiny smiled.

"Let's go and get the girls," Destiny said.

When the two of them reached the craft table, the girls had just finished decorating their ornaments. Both girls used a lot of felt to make small ornaments. They also used a lot of glitter.

"Let's go and hang them on the craft tree," Sapphire said.

"You girls did a wonderful job on your ornaments," Destiny said.

Once they reached the tree, each girl placed their ornaments on the tree.

"It's beautiful," Sapphire said.

"I think it looks perfect with all the handmade ornaments," Holly said.

"Whoever gets this tree is going to love it!" Destiny said.

The raffle was going well for the tree auction. People were very excited as they strolled the grounds, looking at all the Christmas trees and placing their raffle tickets in the boxes.

"You did a wonderful job on the trees, Destiny," Chris said.

"Thank you," Destiny said.

Amber went up on stage and announced the pie-eating contest was about to start if anyone wanted to enter. The winner will get a gold ribbon and a blueberry pie.

"Come on, Daddy, you can win this," Sapphire said.

"Okay, it does sound like fun, and I do like my blueberry pies," he announced.

Six people sat at the table, ready to eat.

"Are you ready?" Amber asked. "Go!"

The pie contest began with the six men going after the pies. It was hysterical to watch them as blueberries were going all over their faces. Luckily, they all had a piece of cloth wrapped around their necks. One of the men was leading with Chris coming in second. *The contest isn't over yet,* Chris thought. People watching were laughing and cheering them on.

"Come on, Chris, you can do it!" Destiny said.

"Come on, Daddy!" Sapphire said, laughing. Holly was cheering him on too.

"The pie is almost gone," Eric announced. "Who's going to be our winner?" Chris took his last bite, stood, and cheered. "The winner of this pie-eating contest is Chris Adams!" Eric said. Everyone cheered. The men all shook one another's hands and congratulated Chris. "For the winner, here is your gold ribbon and blueberry pie," Eric said. The writing on the ribbon said, "I ate the whole thing." Everyone laughed.

"I think that I'll wait on eating this pie," Chris said.

"You do look kind of blue," Daniel said. Everyone laughed.

Once Chris cleaned up, he took Sapphire to the dance floor.

"May I have this dance, my dear?" Chris asked Sapphire.

"Yes, you may," she said as she stood on his two feet, swaying to the music.

Destiny took Holly and held her as they danced. Just as the music was beginning to pick up, all four of them started dancing to the beat.

"I love dancing," Holly said.

"Me too!" Sapphire said.

Destiny saw Amber heading back to the stage. Amber announced the snowman contest.

"Families that want to participate in the snowman contest should gather together in a snowy spot. Once the teams were set, you'll have fifteen minutes to build your snowman. The judges will be Mr. and Mrs. Randall."

"Okay, let's go!" Sapphire said.

"I have to get the items in the truck for the snowman. I'll be right back," Chris said.

"Hurry, Daddy, the contest is about to begin," Sapphire announced.

Team by team, people were getting ready to start the race in building their snowman. Among other teams, Chris, Destiny, Sapphire, and Holly were on one team. Daniel and Paige were on another team.

"Okay, I'm back. Are we ready?" Chris said.

"We're ready!" Destiny yelled.

"Let the snowman contest commence," Amber said as the horn went off.

People watching the snowman contest started cheering on the teams, watching the snow fly about as all the teams were rushed to roll the snow into balls. It was hysterical watching them build their snowman. Everyone was rolling one part of the body after another. Minutes went by as the teams' snowmen began to take form. Paige and Daniel were in the lead. Chris and his team were not far behind but catching up. The fun part of the contest was to see how they decorate the snowmen. People had all kinds of hats, wigs, scarves, and material for the eyes, nose, and mouth. Some brought flowers, sunglasses, brooms, scrawls, and capes. Some even hid some of their props. Just as the one-minute alarm went off, Chris, Destiny, and the girls began dressing up their snowman. They used a black hat, two large blue marble eyes, a long carrot for its nose, and a red licorice for mouth. They also used three large buttons for the front of the snowman and a broom to hold.

The horn went off, and Amber said, "Stop decorating." Amber announced that there would be three ribbon winners—the one that was made the fastest, the most creative, and the most unique. Mr. and Mrs. Randall walked around with a clipboard, checking each snowman. There were so many snowmen that it took a while to tally up the points.

Sapphire looked around at the snowmen and said, "It looks like we have a family of snowmen. They are all so good."

"Some of them are girls and some are boys," Holly said.

"Everyone did a great job," Chris said.

"Yes, they did," Destiny said. "I love Daniel and Paige's snowman."

"Paige is pretty creative," Chris said.

Amber and Eric added up the points and headed toward the stage. "Hello. everyone. Let me tell you, the Randalls had a hard time deciding because they are all so wonderful. Before I announce the winners, I would like to thank the Randalls for helping us out with the snowman contest and for all you that participated," Amber said.

"The first blue ribbon goes to the Johnson family for the most creative. The winner of the most unique yellow ribbon goes to the McGrath family, and the team that made their snowman the fastest goes to Chris, Destiny, Sapphire, and Holly," Amber said as she handed out all the ribbons. Everyone cheered and applauded. Amber asked everyone to stay by their snowman for a photograph.

"That was so much fun!" Sapphire said.

As Amber finished the team's photograph, the music began to play again.

"Let's eat! I'm hungry," Sapphire said.

"Me too!" Holly said.

Chris, Destiny, Virginia, Sapphire, and Holly got in line for the chicken barbecue dinner. Then they went to sit by the bonfire to eat. Daniel and Paige joined them. The music was playing in the background.

"They're a really good band," Paige said.

"They live in town and play at a lot of functions. We're lucky we got them to play," Chris said.

"What is the name of the band?" Destiny asked.

"Sole Searchers," Chris said.

"They're great and can play any genre of music, but my favorite is country songs," Chris announced.

As they were finishing their supper, they all decided to make some s'mores.

"I love toasting marshmallows," Holly said.

"The tricky part of toasting marshmallows is to not burn them," Chris said.

"I like to toast them until they're golden brown," Destiny said.

"I like the dark marshmallow. It gives them some crunch," Daniel said.

"Let's get the graham crackers and chocolate so I can make my s'more," Sapphire said.

Once everyone had their fill of s'mores, Sapphire asked her daddy to dance with her again. Chris led Sapphire to the dance floor, and they began to dance. Destiny and Holly followed suit. It was really sweet to see the parents dancing with their daughters. Destiny looked over at Chris and saw how sweet he was with Sapphire. She understood why she had so many good feelings for him. When Chris finished dancing with Sapphire, he asked Holly to dance. It meant so much to see Chris and Holly relating so well. It warmed Destiny's heart and made her feel even closer to Chris. When the song ended, a faster song began.

"Let's all dance together," Chris suggested to Destiny, Virginia, Sapphire, and Holly.

After a few more songs, Sapphire and Holly wanted to dance with Paige and then have a rest. While they were resting, Sapphire said to her dad, "You and Destiny go dance. We'll watch you." As Sapphire and Holly watched, they could see just how much they liked each other. "I wonder if they're in love," Sapphire said to Holly.

"It sure looks like it. They're so happy together," Holly said.

"It looks like we'll be sisters soon. That's what I want Santa to bring me," Holly said.

"I want that too," Sapphire said. They gave each other a hug.

"I would really like that very much," Holly said with a smile.

"Oh look, there's a shooting star! Let's make a wish!" Sapphire announced to Holly. They each closed their eyes and made their wish. "I hope my wish comes true," Sapphire said.

"I hope that mine comes true too," Holly said.

After the girls made a wish, they went up to Chris and Destiny and asked if they could go and get some hot chocolate. The girls said that they would be right back.

Chris and Destiny stayed on the dance floor and continued to dance.

"I need to tell you something, Destiny. You make me feel like I'm on top of the world. My heart skips a beat whenever I see you. My days seem longer until I can be with you again. You're a wonderful mother. What I am trying to say is that I love you, Destiny!" Chris told her. They gave each other a hug. "I love Holly too! She's a sweet little girl."

"Chris, my heart is so full when I'm with you. I love having you in my life. I see how kind and loving you are to Holly, and it warms my heart. I am grateful for your friendship and love. You mean to world to me, and I want to continue to grow stronger in our relationship. What I'm trying to say to you is that I love you too. And Sapphire means the world to me, and I love her too."

They shared a sweet kiss together and hugged again.

Just as Chris and Destiny finished their conversion, they went and got the girls. Amber got on the stage and announced all the winners of the themed trees. The winners were so excited and went to get their trees. The mistletoe dance became a success, and everyone was having a wonderful time. As the evening came to a close, Amber got back on stage and announced that she had one more surprise for everyone.

"Let me just get off the stage. She went over to Eric and whispered into her husband's ears. Eric got on his phone and was talking to someone on the other end when suddenly, the sky was filled with fireworks.

"What a wonderful way to end the evening," Destiny said.

Everyone was in awe of the beautiful colors that flared up into the sky. There were a lot of oohs and awws and smiles as the fireworks brightened the sky. The finale was gorgeous with streams of colors as the fireworks burst all at once while cheers and hollers ensued.

"What a great night," Chris said.

Just before everyone left, Amber made her last announcement. "I want to thank everyone for coming, and I wish you a good night."

Chris, Destiny, Virginia, Daniel, Paige, Amber, and Eric all stayed to help clean up. When they were finished, everyone went back to their cars and said good night. Chris and Destiny stole a kiss before leaving.

"I'll talk to you tomorrow, Destiny. Good night," Chris said.

Once Destiny tucked Holly into bed, she went to talk to her mother about Chris.

"Mom, tonight was the best night of my life. Chris told me how he feels about me. He told me that he loves me and wants to spend his life with me."

"You two have been getting closer for some time now," Virginia said.

"Our relationship all started because of the fire at my house. It's amazing where fate has brought me," Destiny said. "Mom, I've fallen hard for Chris, and I told him that I was in love with him too."

"Does he love Holly too?" Virginia asked.

"Yes, he loves Holly, and I love Sapphire," she said. "The girls love each other and consider themselves to be best friends."

"I'm happy for you two. I just don't want what happened to you before happen to you again," Virginia said.

"Chris is nothing like my ex, Carl. Chris is handsome, ambitious, strong, kind. He has goals. He treats others kindly and with respect.

He's fun and adventurous. He loves his daughter with all of his heart and soul. In my eyes, he's also loving, supportive, and wants me to reach for my dreams and to be a partner with me through the good times and the bad," Destiny told her mother.

"It sounds like you're making vows," Virginia said with a smile. "I'm happy for all of you. I think that you will have a wonderful life with Chris and Sapphire."

"Me too!"

"It sounds to me that Chris may be proposing soon," Virginia said.

"Maybe," Destiny said with a smile.

"What about your house?" Virginia said.

"I'll take one day at a time. Besides, he hasn't asked me to marry him," Destiny said. "My house is being taken care of by the construction crew, and Holly and I will move back into the house hopefully soon."

"You're a smart young lady, and you will do what's best for you and Holly," Virginia said.

"Holly is my first priority, and I know that she will be happy when the time comes for all of us to be together," Destiny told her mother. "I love you, Mom. Thank you so much for listening to me. You mean to world to me," Destiny said.

"I love you too, Destiny," Virginia told her. "I think that it's time to turn in."

"Good night, Mom," Destiny said as she hugged her mother. "Sweet dreams."

Chapter 9

The next morning, Destiny got up early and went to the town hall. She took all the letters to the soldiers and mailed them out with some homemade cookies, nuts, and magazines and some necessities. Then she went back to the bed-and-breakfast and got Holly before heading to work.

"I love my job! I am truly blessed," Destiny said to Holly as she drove to the florist shop.

"We all had a great time at the mistletoe dance last night," Holly said.

"Yes, we did," Destiny replied. "Holly, can I ask you how you feel about Chris and Sapphire?"

"I really like him and Sapphire too. Chris is very nice to me and is a good daddy. Sapphire is my best friend, but I wish she were my sister."

"I love him, Holly," Destiny said.

"I knew it! Sapphire and I were watching you both dance, and we were hoping that you loved each other," Holly said. "Does he love you, Mommy?"

"Yes, he loves me, but he also loves you," Destiny told her.

"He loves me," Holly said.

"Yes, sweetheart," Destiny said.

"Then maybe I'll have a daddy?" Holly asked.

"I think so." Destiny hugged Holly. "We're beginning to be a family now," Destiny replied to Holly.

"I would like to have a daddy," Holly said with tears in her eyes.

"I know, sweetheart." Destiny thought about talking to Chris about Holly's feeling and seeing if he would talk to her.

' "Sapphire and I want you two to be together so we can all be a family," Holly said. "I even asked Santa for it."

"You did!" Destiny said. "That's a tall order for Santa."

"Santa said that too," Holly said.

"Enough talk for now, Holly. You need to get to your schoolwork, and I need to start making bouquet arrangements and taking phone orders."

The day was a pleasant day for Destiny and Holly. Once work was over, Destiny and Holly went to check on their house. When she arrived, Destiny could see all the work that had been done. She asked one of the carpenters how the house was coming.

"The house is coming along really well," the carpenter told Destiny. "We should be done by the end of the week. You should be in your house for Christmas Eve. We had a great crew of carpenters and even some volunteers from the community that pitched in."

"That's amazing!" Destiny said.

"We'll be in our house for Christmas Eve?" Holly said. "I'm so excited! I can't wait till Sapphire sees my room."

"Let's go back to the B and B and tell everyone," Destiny said happily.

When Destiny and Holly got back to the B and B, Chris and Sapphire were already there, waiting for them to hear the surprise that Amber had for her. Destiny walked in the door, and everyone cheered.

"Did you already hear the news about my house?" Destiny questioned.

"No, but we do have a surprise to tell you," Amber said.

"You go first, Destiny," Chris said with a smile.

"Holly and I stopped by my house to see how it was coming along, and I was told by the carpenter that I should be in my house for Christmas Eve," Destiny said excitedly.

Everyone burst into cheers as they shared a hug with Destiny and Holly.

"Okay," Destiny said, "what's your surprise?"

"Eric and I have been counting the money from the mistletoe dance, and we have raised six thousand dollars for you and Holly to refurnish your house," Amber said happily.

"What!" Destiny said as she ran to give Amber a hug and then to Eric. Tears rolled down her cheek. "I can't thank you enough and to all those that pitched in. It's a night that I will never forget. It has meant so much to me to see such generous, kind, and wonderful people. I will always remember this day."

"Congratulations, Destiny," Chris said with a hug. "You too, Holly," he added as he went and hugged Holly.

"I'm so happy for you!" Sapphire said.

"Congratulations," Daniel said with a hug.

"The timing on your house couldn't be any better," Amber said. "Tomorrow we can go shopping for the furniture, rugs, a television, and whatever you need."

Tears were still in Destiny's eyes as she was still in shock.

"Holly can come too," Amber said.

"Don't forget, Mommy," Holly said, "tomorrow is Saturday. We have to go and read to the dogs."

"Sapphire and I will go with you to read to the dogs, and then we'll go shopping," Chris said.

"I'm so excited!" Destiny said.

"Destiny, good things come out of tragedy," Chris said. "You deserve this and to be happy."

"Amber, will you do me a favor and give me everyone's name and address so I can write thank-you cards," Destiny requested.

"That's a large number of people," Amber said.

"If it takes me a year to thank everyone, it will be well worth it," Destiny said.

"They'll like that," Amber said.

"It's been a long day!" Eric said. "I'm turning in."

"I'll come join you, honey," Amber said.

"I'm going to my bedroom and finish reading my book," Daniel said.

"Girls, you two go play quietly while Destiny and I talk," Chris announced.

"Okay, Daddy," Sapphire said.

"Why don't we make a list of things that you're going to need for the house?" Chris asked.

"Great idea!" Destiny said. "I have been buying some items for the house, so that will help. The first thing I want to do is work on Holly's room. It will bring her so much joy. I want to buy her white furniture, paint her room the color orchid, and get some lace curtains, a lace canopy over her bed, and a lace bedspread. She loves fairies, so I want to make it whimsical for her."

"I can build her a shelf for her snow globes as she gets more and for her other toys," Chris said.

"You would do that for Holly?" Destiny said.

"It's an easy thing to make. It'll only take me an hour, and I'll paint it white," Chris said.

Destiny hugged Chris and told him that she loved him.

"I love you too!" Chris responded.

"Then I'll start on the living room. I want it to be simple but nice," Destiny told Chris. "As for the kitchen, I'm not sure," Destiny said. "Luckily, the kitchen wasn't as bad as I thought it would be. The cabinets weren't destroyed, just blackened from the smoke. I think that we can clean them and restock them with a new dinnerware, bowls, and kitchen utensils. The glass kitchen table, refrigerator, and stove are all right, and they just need some heavy cleaning. If we can't get the smoke out of them, then I'll have to buy new ones. I'd like to at least try to clean them," Destiny said.

"Let's see what else you would need," Chris said.

"My bedroom," Destiny said. "Again, I just want my room to be simple too. I'll like it to have that relaxing feel when you walk in. I'll paint a sunset, palm trees, and the ocean on one wall and a light blue on all the other walls. I'm sure that I can find a rippling fountain, some uplifting words to put over my headboard, and some flowering plants. I'm so excited about tomorrow!"

Suddenly, Holly came into the living and said that Sapphire fell asleep on the bed.

"Okay, I guess that's a clue to get her home and into bed. I'll talk to you tomorrow," Chris said to Destiny. "Good night, Holly."

"I'll see you tomorrow," Destiny said.

"Bye, Chris," Holly said.

The next morning, Destiny and Holly got up early for breakfast and got dressed for the day. When they went into the kitchen, Chris and Sapphire were just pulling into the driveway.

"Everyone, ready?" Chris asked.

"Yes," Holly said. "Let's go!"

Everyone got into Destiny's Mustang and headed off to the shelter. The morning went off as planned, and they all had a very pleasant morning reading to the dogs. Then they grabbed some lunch and met Amber downtown.

"I'm so glad that we all can shop together. Now I know that there's a big sale in the attic, so let's start there," Amber said to Destiny.

One piece of furniture was purchased after another, and before Destiny knew it, she had gotten everything on her list. The furniture company said that they would hold the furniture for a week so she could do the painting and fix the house up a bit before the furniture delivery.

"This was a great day!" Destiny said.

Destiny was happy to learn that she didn't use all the charity money that was given to her and told Amber that she would like to donate the rest of it to a homeless shelter.

"My heart is so full, and I am so grateful for this day. It is such a blessing," Destiny said.

"Christmas Eve is coming in four days, and we want to be ready to paint the house when the construction crew is done," Chris said.

"I love my new bed, Mommy," Holly said.

"I'm so glad," Destiny told her.

"So let's go to the hardware store and get all the paint and brushes that we need for the house," Chris said.

The next morning, Destiny got a call from one of the carpenters, and she was told that if she wanted to go to the house and paint, two of the rooms were ready. Destiny was so excited. She called Chris and told him. He said that he would be right over.

Destiny asked Virginia, "If Holly could stay here while Chris and I go and paint the two rooms, it would be great."

"I'd love to watch Holly," Virginia she said.

"I'll call Chris to see if Sapphire can come over too."

"That's great!" Destiny said.

"I think that Virginia, Eric, and I can take the girls to the carousel museum. There's some beautiful replicas of some older animals that used to be in a circus carousel. The girls will love riding the new one that they installed a month ago. I do love riding the carousel. It brings the kid out in me," Amber said.

"Sounds great!" Destiny said.

"We're going to ride a carousel?" Holly said in excitement. "I can't wait!"

Soon, Chris arrived with Sapphire. Amber, Eric, and Virginia were waiting outside with Holly, ready to go.

"See you folks later," Eric said as he waved her hand.

Chris and Destiny loaded up Chris's truck and headed to the house. When they got there, the carpenter showed them the two rooms that were ready for painting. Destiny was happy to see that the rooms were her bedroom and Holly's.

"Let's get the orchid paint and paint all four of her walls. I found a small mural of fairies that we can place on one of her walls. She's going to love it!" Destiny said.

While Destiny was painting up high on the wall, she slipped and fell on the floor, getting paint on her pants. Luckily, there was a tarp on the floor. Then she laughed.

Chris laughed, and Destiny went over and placed some paint on his cheek. Then the painting became a free for all. Paint was brushed everywhere on Chris and Destiny.

One of the carpenters walked into the room after hearing some laughter and just stared at them. "Are you two painting the walls or each other?" the carpenter asked.

"Sorry," Destiny said to the carpenter. "I guess it just got out of hand."

They both went to clean up and started painting Holly's room again. Once Holly's room was painted, Chris and Destiny started painting Destiny's room.

"I really like this shade of light blue," Destiny said. "It'll look good with the ocean mural that I'm going to paint."

"It's nice," Chris said. "Now we have to behave so that we can finish your bedroom today too, "Chris said.

It was early evening when Chris and Destiny finished painting the two rooms.

"The rooms look great!" Destiny said.

"They sure do," Chris said.

When they were getting ready to leave, the carpenter said that they needed another day and then the kitchen, living room, and bathroom would be ready to paint.

"What great news. Thank you so much!" Destiny told the carpenter.

When they arrived back at the B and B, Virginia, Amber, Eric, and the girls were eating supper.

"What's for supper?" Chris asked.

"Pot roast, mashed potatoes, butternut squash, rolls, and apple pie for dessert," Eric said. "Grab yourself a plate, and come join us."

"How was your day?" Chris said, talking to Sapphire and Holly.

"We saw the most beautiful carousel animals," Sapphire said.

Holly said, "We even got to ride on a carousel with the music playing. It sounded so pretty."

"Don't forget to tell them about the café," Amber said.

"Oh, I forgot," Sapphire said. "There was a pretty carousel café there with delicious food. The names of the food were funny like Zebra fries, monkey sticks, tiger roars burger, and an elephant splash."

"Don't forget about the peacock sundae," Holly said.

"What are monkey sticks and a peacock sundae?" Chris asked.

"Monkey sticks are mozzarella sticks, and peacock sundae is vanilla ice cream with colored sprinkles," said Holly.

Everyone laughed.

"I'm glad everyone had a great time today," Chris said.

"How did the painting go?" Virginia asked, noticing the paint on their clothes.

"We did get two rooms painted," Chris said.

"I have some more great news," Destiny said. "We can go back in another day to do some more painting."

"That's great, Mommy!" Holly said. "How's my room coming?"

"It's very pretty, but you'll have to wait because I want you to be surprised," Destiny told her daughter.

"Speaking of more work, I have to go and get some things done at home. So Sapphire and I have to head out," Chris announced. "Good night, everyone."

Destiny walked Chris and Sapphire to their truck.

"Will I see you tomorrow?" Destiny asked.

"Sure, after work. Why don't you and Holly come over my house for dinner?"

"I'd love to. Good night, Sapphire. See you two tomorrow," Destiny said. Destiny went back into the house and played with Holly.

When Chris got home, he brought Dakota into his barn and worked on Holly's shelf while Sapphire watched. Chris added some special touches to her shelf. He engraved her name on the front of the shelf and then painted the whole shelf.

"It's beautiful, Daddy. Holly is going to love it!" Sapphire said happily.

"Remember, it's a surprise!" Chris told Sapphire.

"Don't worry, I won't tell her," Sapphire said. "Daddy, can I go to bed? I'm so tired," Sapphire told him.

"Sure, sweetie. Let me just clean up while you get your pajamas on, and then I'll read you a bedtime story," Chris said. "Do you know how much I love you, Sapphire? I love you to the moon and back."

"I love you too, Daddy, to the moon and back," Sapphire said. "Thanks for the bedtime story."

"Good night, my princess!" Chris said with a kiss to her forehead. Chris went out to the living room to watch some sports and relax before going to bed.

Chapter 10

The next morning went as usual. Breakfast was made. Chris and Sapphire got ready for their day. Sapphire played with Dakota for a bit, rubbing her tummy. Paige came to get Sapphire on and off the bus. Chris called Destiny with a fun idea.

"What do you say that we take the girls to the ice castle? There's one about an hour from here. It would be magical for the girls. It's nice during the day, but at night, the ice castle lights up."

"It sounds like a great idea!" Destiny said.

"We want to dress in extra warm clothing as everything is made of ice and snow and it's really cold," Chris said.

"Well, why don't we go around four o'clock so we can enjoy showing the girls the castle during the day? Then when it gets dark, we can enjoy the colorful lights in the castle," Destiny said.

"We'll tell the girls later," Chris said.

"This is going to be so much fun!" Destiny said. "I'm sure that my mom would love to go too."

"If you don't mind, I'd like to invite my parents, Daniel, and Paige," Chris asked.

"Of course! Let's make it a family day," Destiny announced.

"Sounds great, Destiny. Well, I have to get to work. Have a wonderful day, Destiny," Chris said.

"You too," Destiny replied.

The day went by quickly, and before they knew it, Chris and Sapphire were on their way to the bed-and-breakfast. Everyone, still being in the Christmas mood, was singing carols when Chris and Sapphire walked in.

"Merry Christmas!" Chris shouted as he closed the door.

Daniel and Paige were sitting on the couch, enjoying each other's company and looking pretty comfy.

"How're things going, Daniel?" Chris asked.

"Things are going just great!" Daniel said. "I have made a decision. I have decided to come back home for good. I'll find an apartment downtown. I like being a mechanic, and I should be able to find a job here in Alaska. I also kind of like this lady next to me and want to see more of her," Daniel said as he touched Paige's hand. Paige was excited that he had made that commitment to her and blushed a little.

"You know my offer still stands. You can come work for me," Chris said.

"I thank you for the offer," Daniel said, "but I enjoy working on cars, and I'm good at it."

"You can stay with us till you get settled," Amber said.

"Let's celebrate Daniel on moving back to Alaska," Eric said.

"A toast," Chris said. "May you always find joy and happiness in your life, and may it continue to bring you closer to your hopes and dreams."

"I have a great way we can celebrate the holidays together. Let's all go to the ice castle!" Chris announced.

"I've heard it's a wonderful place to visit," Paige said. "I'm in."

"I'm in too," Daniel said.

"I want to go!" Sapphire said.

"Me too!" Holly announced.

"Mom, would you like to go?"

"I'd love to," Virginia said.

"Eric and I are in. When are we going?" Amber said.

"Why not leave now? We can grab a bite to eat on our way there," Chris said.

"Great idea!" Destiny said. "Ready, Mom?" Destiny asked her mother.

"Let's go!" Virginia replied. "This is going to be fun."

They all got dressed in extra warm clothes and then got into their vehicles and headed out. It was a pretty day with the sun shining brightly on the snow.

"I can't wait till we get there," Holly said.

"Me too," Sapphire said. About a half hour later, Sapphire asked, "Are we there yet?"

"Almost," Chris said. "We're halfway there."

"Why don't you girls read a book?" Chris asked. "I have some in the back pouch of the truck."

"I'll read you a story," Sapphire told Holly.

"I love stories!" Holly replied.

When everyone arrived at the ice castle, they parked their cars and headed toward the gate. There was a long line of people waiting to get into the ice castle. Once everyone passed through the gate, they saw that everything was made of ice and snow, even the walking paths. A sign in front of the ice castle said that there were roughly ten thousand icicles placed throughout the ice castle. The water helps freeze the castle. In time, the icicles get absorbed into the ice structure.

"Look, Mommy," Holly said, "the ice is blue!"

"So pretty," Sapphire said. "Why is the ice blue?" Sapphire asked.

Eric said, "Ice is blue for the same reason the ocean is blue. Ice has the same color properties of water, and the thicker the ice, the deeper shade of blue the ice becomes."

"That's interesting," Daniel said.

"The structure of the castle," Chris said, "is sprayed with water over wooden frames to create the castle. The more icicles that form over the structure, the more magical it appears."

"We have to be careful of our walking in the slush," Virginia said. "We don't want to fall."

"Look, there are several tunnels we can crawl through and slide on," Amber said.

Inside the castle were beautiful tall blue walls. There was a lot of room to move from one area to the next. Each room had its own special feature that made it stand out from the other rooms. There was one big open room in the center of the castle where there was a large fountain that sprayed upward and changed color from blue to yellow to orange and to green. There were a lot of people taking photographs. It was so beautiful there.

"Let's climb these steps and slide to the bottom," Sapphire said. Chris and Destiny went with them.

"Thank goodness, we had a mat to sit on going down the slide," Destiny said.

"Let's go down the slide again. That was fun!" Holly said.

"Let's do it again," Sapphire announced.

"I'll watch the girls," Virginia said. "Why don't you go check out the balcony and I'll wait here with the girls?"

While Chris and Destiny had a moment, Chris wanted to give Destiny a gift. Once they got to the balcony, Chris pulled something out of his pocket and handed it to Destiny with a kiss.

Chris said, "I've been wanting to give you something to show you how much I care and love you." Destiny opened the blue box to find a beautiful crystal heart necklace with a cardinal inside and a message on the back that says, "To my dear Destiny. May we always fly together."

"I absolutely love it! Thank you so much!" Destiny said as she hugged Chris. A tear ran down her cheek.

"You're so welcome," Chris said as he put the necklace around Destiny's neck.

Destiny was so excited to show it to everyone. Chris and Destiny went back to the girls.

"Did you girls have fun sliding?" Destiny asked.

"It was a blast," Holly said.

"I loved it!" Sapphire said.

Destiny went over to her mother and showed her the necklace.

"What a lovely necklace," Virginia said as she came closer to look at it.

"My son has good taste," Amber said. "It's very lovely."

"Mommy, it's very pretty," Holly said. "especially with the cardinal inside."

"I love the heart shape and the pretty cardinal inside." Sapphire spoke out.

"I love it so much!" Destiny said as she held on to the necklace.

As the evening skies were becoming darker, the ice castle began to glow in many colors. The icicles were changing colors. Even the blocks of ice in the center of the castle were lighting up and changing colors. Holly and Sapphire were jumping from one block to the other.

"These blocks are so pretty," Sapphire said.

"It's magical," Paige said, holding on to Daniel's hand.

"I'm so glad that we came when we did," Destiny said.

"The castle belongs in a fairy-tale story," Holly said.

"It's very lovely," Amber said.

"Let's have some hot chocolate and a hot cinnamon roll before we go," Virginia said.

"I'm so glad that they offer something hot to drink," Amber said.

"Hmmm, this hot cocoa is delicious," Paige said.

"It's been a wonderful evening, but it's time we all head home," Eric said.

Everyone agreed and headed home.

"Destiny, would you and Holly like to stay over?" Chris asked.

"How about it, Holly? Would you like to sleep over Sapphire's house?" Destiny asked.

"Can we, Mommy, please?" Holly asked.

"Let's do it!" Destiny said.

Sapphire hugged Holly and was very happy to have her sleep over.

Once Chris, Destiny, and the girls arrived home, Chris let Dakota out, and then they all sat on the swing, talking about the evening at the ice castle and how much fun they had. Even Dakota was having fun running around. It was a beautiful night. Everyone was enjoying the starry night.

"Let's play fetch with Dakota," Chris said.

"Go get it!" Sapphire said, throwing the stick.

"She's fast!" Holly said.

"She likes this game," Sapphire said.

Once they tired Dakota out and tired themselves out, they all sat back on the swing.

"Look at the stars," Destiny said.

"The stars are so bright," Sapphire said.

"Oh look," Destiny said, "there's a shooting star!"

"Everyone needs to make a wish," Holly said.

"I made my wish," Chris said.

"I don't need anything. I have everything I want right here," Destiny said as she hugged the girls and Chris.

"Destiny, do you mind if I spend some time with Holly?" Chris asked.

"Sure, I'd like some time with Sapphire alone too," Destiny said.

Chris took Holly's hand, and they went into the barn and talked.

"You know, Holly, I care about you and your mom so much," Chris said. "I love you both."

"I know," Holly said. "I'm glad that you and my mommy are happy. I'm glad that you love me too."

"I think that when the time is right, we will all become a real family," Chris said.

"I told my mommy that I would like to have you as my daddy," Holly said.

"I would love to be your daddy," Chris said. "You are a very special young lady. Can you sit on the bale of hay while I go and get something in the back of the barn?" Chris asked.

"Okay," Holly said.

"I made you something for your bedroom, and I hope that you like it."

"What is it?" Holly asked.

Chris uncovered the shelf and brought it over to Holly.

"You made this for me? I love it, and it has my name on it. Thank you for the shelf. It's beautiful," Holly said as she hugged Chris.

"It's something to put your snow globes on and your books."

"All my snow globes got thrown away," Holly said.

"Well, I'd like to take care of that," Chris said as he picked a box that he had and handed it to Holly. "Here's something, Holly, to start your new collection," Chris said. Holly opened the box and pulled out a snow globe.

"It has a castle and a fairy inside with glitter that swirls around," Holly said. "It even plays music. I love it!" Holly said excitedly. "You're the best!"

"What do you say that we go and show your mommy?" Chris said.

While Chris was talking to Holly, Destiny took the opportunity to talk to Sapphire.

"Sapphire, I want you to know that I love you and Chris very much. I want to be here for you whenever you need me. You are a very special girl, and I want to make us a family," Destiny said.

"I like the idea of you being my mommy," Sapphire said.

"I want to make you happy too," Destiny told Sapphire.

"I am happy," she said.

"Down the road, I hope that we can be a real family," Destiny said.

"I would like to have a mommy, and I think that you would be a wonderful mommy for me," Sapphire said as she hugged Destiny.

"I'll do the best I can every day to make you feel special," Destiny said.

"Can you stay here for a moment?" She went to the back of the truck and took out a big bag. Destiny came back and sat next to Sapphire and told her that she knew that she loved animals. "So I got this for you," Destiny said.

"When did you get this?" Sapphire asked, not seeing anything in the truck when she was in it. Sapphire opened the bag and took out a large stuffed brown bear.

"I love it!" Sapphire said. "It reminds me of a story I was once told, how a mother bear took care of this lost child and then returned the child to its mother."

"That's a cute story," Destiny said.

"Thank you so much!" Sapphire said as she hugged Destiny.

Chris and Holly were coming back with the shelf and snow globe to show Sapphire and Destiny.

"Did you two have a nice talk?" Destiny asked them.

"We had a nice talk, and look at what Chris made for me," Holly said.

"It's beautiful!" Destiny said.

"I watched my daddy make the shelf the other day in the barn, "Sapphire said. "He did a great job on it."

"He sure did," Destiny said.

Then Holly showed her mommy the snow globe.

"Wow! This is a beautiful snow globe. We will have to take extra care of this until we can get it on the shelf," Destiny's said.

"Daddy, look at the bear that Destiny got me!"

"It's awesome!" Chris stated. "I think that it's time for you two young ladies to get some sleep," Chris said to the girls.

Chris and Destiny tucked the girls into bed and wished them sweet dreams.

"Let's sit by the fire," Chris said.

"You know," Destiny said, "we really are beginning to feel like a family," Destiny said as she held his hands.

"I really like it too," Chris said.

"Thank you for the beautiful necklace and Holly's gifts," Destiny said. "You are going to make a great dad for Holly."

"Thank you for Sapphire's gift," Chris said.

"You're welcome," Destiny said. "When I saw it in the store, I had to get it and sneak into the back of your truck. I'm glad she didn't see it."

"You are very loving and kind to Sapphire," Chris said. "It makes me so happy. She needs a mother who will be gentle, loving, and patient with her."

"Thank you," Destiny said.

Suddenly, Destiny got a call from the contractor, telling her that she could finish painting the last set of rooms and that they were done with all the repairs on the house. Destiny told Chris the good news.

"I'll tell the girls in the morning," Destiny said.

"We should call it a night so we can get an early start on the painting," Chris said.

"Just as Destiny was getting ready for bed, Holly came in and said that she had a bad dream. Destiny said good night to Chris and then went to lay down with Holly."

When morning arrived, Holly and Sapphire were playing with the dolls. Destiny awoke as she heard their giggles.

"Good morning, princesses," Destiny said. "Why don't you two go and wake up Chris?"

"Wake up! Wake up!" Sapphire and Holly said as they tickled him.

"Okay! Okay! I'm awake, you little monkeys," Chris said, laughing. "I'm going to get you!" he said as he chased the girls into the kitchen.

"We win! We win! We beat you!" Sapphire announced. Destiny walked in all dressed, ready to go to her house.

"I'm going to take Dakota for a quick run, and I'll be right back," Chris said. "You girls go get ready to head to Destiny's house."

When Chris came back, he asked everyone if they were ready to go.

"I'll see you later," Chris said to Dakota, patting her head.

"Let's all grab some breakfast and run," Destiny said.

"Run where?" Holly asked with a giggle.

"I have some good news, Holly. We can finish painting the house," Destiny said.

"I'm so happy," Holly said. "We'll be able to go back home!"

"If I can get the living room, dining room, and bathrooms painted and sorted out, then we can move back in on Christmas Eve."

"I'm so happy for you," Sapphire said.

"Thank you," Destiny responded.

"Can I help?" Holly asked.

"You and Sapphire can, but I want you to bring some toys to play with to keep yourselves busy."

Everyone grabbed some granola bars, bananas, and drinks to go. When they arrived at the house, the first thing that Holly wanted to do was see her room.

"It's beautiful!" Holly said. "I love the color of my room. Thanks, Mommy!"

"You're welcome, but just wait till you see your room all decorated. You'll really love your room."

"Before we begin to paint, we need to scrub the table, cabinets, stove, and refrigerator."

This process took a few hours, but it seemed to work; the smoke smell was gone. Then the painting began.

After playing for a few hours, Sapphire and Holly asked Destiny if they could paint too.

"Okay, girls. I bought you some smocks to wear while your painting," Destiny said. Chris went into the closet and grabbed some more paint, and everyone began painting.

"This is fun!" Sapphire said.

"It sure is," Holly said.

After an hour, Destiny noticed quite a lot of paint on the girls' smocks and in their hair.

"Okay, girls," Destiny said, "I think that you should go and clean up and then go play." The morning seemed to fly by as Destiny and Chris finished the last of the walls.

"This looks great!" Destiny said.

"It sure does," Chris remarked.

"I'm so happy," Destiny said as she hugged Chris.

Chris said, "Let's give the paint a day to dry, and then tomorrow after work, I can help you start moving your things in."

"I'm only working half the day," Destiny said.

"Christmas Eve is one of my busiest times, but I'm sure the staff can handle the tree lot for a little while."

The next day arrived. Destiny had called the furniture company to come and deliver the furniture. It was such an exciting day for Destiny and Holly.

When Destiny and Holly arrived at their house, they began to decorate the rooms and tried to finish before the furniture came. When Chris arrived, he brought Destiny and Holly as a surprise. It was a Christmas tree.

"Oh, thank you. It's beautiful!" Destiny said as Chris lugged it into the house.

"We brought some decorations and lights too!" Sapphire said.

"I also brought my parents and Daniel to help carry the furniture," Chris said. "We can finish decorating the rooms once all the furniture is in and set up."

Once the furniture arrived, everyone chipped in, and within an hour, all the furniture was in place.

"I love my bedroom!" Holly said. "It has a fairy theme."

"It's all so beautiful," Amber said. "The rooms look so nice. You did a great job painting too."

"I call it simply elegant," Destiny said. "I also want to say thank you, everyone, for helping me today."

Once the house was finished, everyone sat and enjoyed a nice lunch that Destiny made.

"Can we decorate the tree now?" Holly asked.

"I'm so excited that today is Christmas Eve!" Sapphire said.

"Me too!" Holly said.

Once the tree was in place, everyone sang Christmas carols as they decorated the tree.

"Will Santa know that we're here now?" Holly said.

"He always knows where you are," Destiny replied.

"Oh good!" Holly said, relieved.

"What do you want to do for Christmas Eve?" Destiny asked Holly.

"Oh, we have a Christmas Eve dinner at my house tonight at six o'clock. I would love it if you and Holly come," Amber said.

"We would love to go," Destiny said.

"Can I wear my new Christmas dress that you bought yesterday?" Holly asked.

"You certainly can," Destiny told her.

"Well, I need to get home so I can start the Christmas Eve dinner. All the visitors at the B and B will be there as well. See you all later," Amber said as she, Eric, and Daniel left.

"Would you like my help?" Destiny asked.

"No, thank you. You just enjoy your time at home, and I'll see you at six."

"This has been a great day!" Destiny said.

"And it's going to get even better," Chris said.

"Oh yeah? What are you up to now, Chris?" Destiny asked.

"I don't know," Chris said with a smirk.

"Mommy, me and Sapphire are going to play in my room," Holly said.

"Just for another hour. Then we need to go home and get ready for the Christmas Eve dinner," Chris said.

"Okay, Daddy," Sapphire said.

"It feels so good to relax and just enjoy the view," Chris said, gazing at Destiny.

"Chris, it sure does feel good to see that all the work we've done come to fruition."

"Holly is pretty happy too," Chris said.

"Yes, she is," Destiny said.

An hour passed when Sapphire and Chris had to go home to get ready for the Christmas Eve dinner.

"See you both soon," Destiny said as she and Holly waved goodbye.

Chapter 11

"Holly, let's get you into your Christmas dress," Destiny said.

"Okay, Mommy," Holly said as she skipped to her bedroom.

"You look so beautiful, Holly," Destiny said.

Her dress was red-and-green plaid on the bottom of her dress with a red top and a red ribbon going around her waist. Destiny fixed Holly's hair and added a small red flower.

"Now you need to get dressed, Mommy," Holly said.

"I think that I'll wear my red chiffon dress with the necklace Chris gave me," Destiny said.

Once they were all set to go, they headed out to the B and B.

"Let's go, Mommy," Holly said.

Once Destiny and Holly arrived, they went out to the living room. Many of the guests were already there, enjoying their cocktails.

Chris and Sapphire walked into the house all dressed up too. Chris was in a dark gray suit, and Sapphire had a beautiful red dress with a white sash around her waist.

"You two look absolutely gorgeous," Amber said. "Why don't you go and mingle with the others and enjoy some appetizers?"

Chris and Sapphire walked into the living room and said, "Merry Christmas, everyone."

Chris took Destiny's hand and said, "You look stunning."

"You look pretty handsome yourself," Destiny said as she hugged Chris.

"Look, Daddy, she's wearing the necklace you got her," Sapphire said.

"Yes, I am," Destiny said. "Sapphire, you look very pretty."

"Thank you," she said. Sapphire went over to Holly and said, "You look pretty. I like your dress."

"I like your dress too," Holly told her.

Suddenly, Paige came walking into the room. She looked beautiful in her green dress and her hair in an updo style. She saw Sapphire and Holly and smiled and waved. Her eyes scanned the room, looking for Daniel. When she spotted him, she walked by Chris, Destiny, Sapphire, and Holly, wishing them a Merry Christmas, and then went to Daniel. Daniel hugged her, and they had a seat with Chris and Destiny.

Once everyone was there, the Christmas Eve dinner began. It was like a royal dinner with everything looking so elegant and smelling great. It was an exquisite buffet lined up along the two tables that were set up for the meal.

"Amber, you did a spectacular job on this meal," Destiny voiced.

"It's amazing, Mom," Chris said.

"Thank you," Amber said. "Eric was a big help. He loves to cook."

Just as the meal was ready to be served, Eric asked for everyone to get a glass of sparkling cider so they could make a toast.

Eric said, "Let's raise our glasses," as he began the toast. "Thank you all for coming to our Christmas Eve dinner. May your hearts be filled with joy this holiday season. May you all have good health, the love of family and friends. May we always remember the true meaning of Christmas and keep it in our hearts, minds, and souls. Merry Christmas!"

"Merry Christmas!" everyone shouted with glee.

"Let's eat!" Amber announced.

The feast began as everyone lined up for the buffet. The food included a roasted turkey, baked ham, stuffing, mashed potatoes, butternut squash, turnips, acorn squash, green bean casserole, fresh corn, brown rice, salad, fruit cups, deviled eggs, gravy, homemade bread and butter, and cranberry sauce.

"There are so many things to choose from it's hard to decide. I'll just get a little of everything," Destiny said.

"I love to eat!" Chris said. "My mom is a great cook."

"I know," Destiny said with a smile.

"Now, girls," Destiny said, "I want you two to eat a nice dinner and no desserts until you're done with your meal."

"I will. I love Grandma's cooking!" Sapphire said.

"Me too," Holly said.

"Everything looks delicious, Amber," Virginia voiced as she sat at the table.

As everyone sat and enjoyed their meal, you could see how much fun everyone was having by the smiles on their faces. The dessert table was set up after the leftovers were packaged and put into the refrigerator. The desserts included a cake to celebrate Christ's birth; brownies; apple, blueberry, cherry, chocolate cream, and banana cream pie cheesecakes; cupcakes; and a variety of cookies and candies.

"I think after eating this food, I need a nap," Chris said.

"I agree," Daniel said.

"I'm going to do an extra workout tomorrow." Destiny laughed.

"Let's just enjoy everything today and worry about it tomorrow," Amber chuckled.

When everyone finished the desserts, Amber suggested that everyone sing Christmas carols and then they would open their Christmas stockings. Chris got his guitar and began playing. People were filled with so much joy and happiness. You could hear it in everyone's singing. Once the singing ended, each guest had a stocking filled with little surprises. It was a pleasant surprise for everyone. The faces were precious as everyone found their stocking and began to go through it. The smiles warmed everyone's heart. Most of the gifts were homemade hats and gloves made by Amber. Every year she worked on her knitting projects to get ready for the coming Christmas. Amber loved to bring so much joy to her guests.

Just as Destiny left the room to check on Holly and Sapphire, Chris whispered to Daniel, "I need your help, Daniel," Chris said. "Come follow me," he said as they grabbed their jackets and went out the door. "I need your help with a present for Destiny," Chris said.

Chris and Daniel went out to their parents' barn to work on Destiny's surprise gift.

"I think this is the perfect time to tell Destiny just how much she means to me. I love her. I want to be with her every day and for the rest of my life," Chris said. "I think that tonight is the perfect time to do the proposal. I'm nervous and excited all at the same time. Here's what we're going to do," Chris said to Daniel.

"This is a great idea!" Daniel said.

"Destiny wouldn't expect this coming," Chris said. "Let's get to work."

Destiny came out of the room and asked Paige, "Where did the guys go?"

"I don't know," Paige said. "They just said that they would be back in a while." Destiny and Paige walked around, mingling with the guests, while the two were away.

A half hour later, Daniel came into the house using a dolly with a large wrapped present placed on it. He placed it by the tree and went to join Paige.

"Where's Chris?" Destiny asked Daniel.

"He's out splitting more wood for the fire," Daniel said with a smile. He had to fib so Destiny would be surprised.

Paige whispered into Daniel's ears and said, "What's going on?"

Daniel whispered back, "You'll see."

"My goodness, who is that present for?" Amber said. Amber walked up to the large present and saw that it had Destiny's name on it and no guess of who it was from.

"Oh my!" Destiny said. "I guess I'll have to wait to open it tomorrow."

"No!" Daniel said. "We all want to see what you got."

"Shouldn't I wait for Chris?" Destiny asked.

"He'll be in momentarily," Daniel said.

"What is it, Mommy?" Holly asked.

"I don't know," Destiny replied.

"Come on, Mommy, open it!"

Destiny began to open it slowly as she didn't want to break anything. Destiny was thinking that maybe it was something for her house.

Just as she began to open the top of the box, Chris popped out.

"It's you!" Destiny was laughing hysterically, hugging him.

Just as Chris was getting out of the box, he lifted his guitar and began to sing a love song that he had written for Destiny. It was very sweet as tears ran down Destiny's cheek. The song expressed his eternal love for Destiny. Destiny was speechless. As Chris finished his song, he got down on one knee and asked Destiny the most important question of her life. He pulled out a ring box from his pocket and asked.

"I love you, Destiny Wright. Would you do me the honor of becoming my wife?"

"YES! YES!" Destiny said as she kissed and hugged him. Everyone cheered. Chris slid a heart-shaped diamond ring on her finger. "It's beautiful, Chris!" Destiny said.

"Mommy! Mommy!" Holly said. "I am so happy. You're getting married!"

"Now I can call you mommy!" Sapphire said to Destiny with a hug.

"And I have a daddy!" Holly said as she went up to Chris and hugged him.

Virginia went up to Destiny with tears in her eyes, hugging her, and said, "I'm so happy for you, my dear." Then turning to Chris, she said, "Welcome to my family. Congratulations, Chris."

"What a momentous occasion to celebrate! I am so happy," said Amber as she hugged her son and Destiny. Then she hugged Holly and said, "Welcome to the family!" Eric came over to hug his son and his soon-to-be daughter-in-law.

"Hold on, everyone," Chris said. "I have one more thing to do."

He pulled out a necklace out of his coat jacket. Chris turned to the girls and gave Sapphire and Holly a necklace where the heart was broken in half. One side was engraved with "My best friend" and the other half said, "We're sisters."

"I love it!" Holly said as she hugged Chris with a tear in her eye.

"It's beautiful!" Sapphire said as she hugged her dad. Then the girls showed each other their halves and put the heart together.

"Yes, we will always be best friends and sisters," Holly said as she hugged Sapphire.

All the guests in the room were all coming to congratulate Destiny and Chris. Paige went up to Chris and Destiny to hug them. "I'm so happy for you both," Paige said.

Daniel said, "Good job, brother!"

"Thanks for your help in pulling off the proposal," Chris said as he hugged his brother. "What a great night! I am the happiest man on earth," Chris announced.

"I'm so elated and so surprised that you did this!" Destiny said.

The Christmas Eve dinner now became a party where everyone was feeling festive as they celebrated the engagement.

Sapphire and Holly went to go and play in Holly's room. While there, they were both talking about how happy their wishes had come true, that Sapphire's dad and Holly's mom would be getting married.

"It's a magical story," Holly said, "just like one of my stories."

Back in the living room, Chris asked Destiny if they could go and talk outside on the swing. While there, Chris asked her when she would like to get married.

"I don't want to wait. I want you to be my wife as soon as possible," Chris said.

"How about New Year's Eve?" Destiny said.

"Yes," Chris said, elated.

Chris stood and hugged Destiny and then swirled her around in happiness. Destiny laughed with joy.

"Why don't we go inside and tell everyone?" Chris asked.

"Okay, let's go!" Destiny replied.

As the party was dying down, Chris called his family, Paige, Holly, and Virginia into the kitchen.

"Destiny and I have some wonderful news," Chris said. "You tell them, Destiny."

"Chris and I have decided to get married on New Year's Eve," Destiny told them.

"So soon," Amber said.

"Well, there's no time to waste," Virginia said.

"We have so much to do," Destiny declared.

"No worries, dear, we can handle this," Amber said. "Christmas Eve was wonderful, and I'm so excited about you and Destiny's future," Amber said to Chris.

"Me too, Mom. Me too," Chris said.

"It's been an exciting day, but I think it's time to call it a night. You have to get Sapphire to bed so Santa can come. We'll talk tomorrow, Chris."

"Okay, Sapphire, are you ready to go home?" Chris asked.

"I sure am tired. It's been a fun Christmas Eve," Sapphire said.

"Before we go, let me say good night to Destiny and Holly." Chris went over to Destiny and gave her a good night kiss. Then he helped Destiny and Holly to her car. "Sweet dreams to my beauties," Chris said.

"Good night, Chris," Destiny said.

"Good night, everyone," Virginia said.

Once Destiny, Virginia, and Holly got home, Destiny put on Holly's pajamas.

Destiny said, "Let's get you ready for bed."

Holly said, "Santa's coming. I have to go to sleep. Good night, Mommy."

"Good night, my sweet little girl."

Virginia came to ask if she could read Holly a bedtime story.

"I would like that, Grandma," Holly said.

Destiny sat on the bed while her mom read the story to Holly. Once Virginia finished reading Holly a fairy tale, she kissed Holly good night.

"That was really sweet of you," Destiny said. "You know that I'm really going to miss you when you go home."

"I'll miss you too," Virginia said.

Destiny got ready for bed and just thought about the wonderful Christmas Eve dinner. She looked at her diamond ring and felt such love from Chris. He put so much effort in making her proposal special. A tear ran down her cheek. She thought, *I am so blessed.* Relaxing on her bed, Destiny fell asleep.

Chapter 12

"It's Christmas! It's Christmas, Mommy! Wake up!" Holly said, jumping on her bed.

"Good morning, sunshine. Merry Christmas," Destiny said as she grabbed her bathrobe and walked out to the living room with Holly.

"Look at all the presents, Mommy!" Holly said excitedly.

"Santa has been good to you," Destiny said. "Would you like to have breakfast?"

"No, thank you," Holly said. "I'm too excited to eat. Let's open our presents."

Once Destiny and Holly opened their presents, Holly played for a while in her room. Holly was very happy that she got three more snow globes, a fairy doll, some books, and some pretty clothes. Destiny found a box under the tree with her name on it. It was from Chris. She unwrapped the gift to find a wooden block written with the words "I love you." It was very sweet. Holly came out of her bedroom and announced that she made her mom a present.

"Look, Mommy, I made you a present. It's a drawing of our new family," Holly said.

"I love it! I'll frame it and hang it on the living room wall," Destiny said with a tear in her eyes. "Thank you, Holly!" Destiny said as she hugged her daughter.

Destiny looked at the clock and realized that she and Holly needed to get ready to head out.

"Mom," Destiny asked, "are you ready?"

"I'll be right there," Virginia replied.

"Holly," Destiny said, "we need to get dressed and head over to the B and B. They are waiting for us." They all got dressed for Christmas Day and headed over to Amber and Eric's house. "Merry Christmas, everyone," Destiny said to her mom, Amber, Eric, and Daniel.

"Merry Christmas!" Holly said.

"How are you two doing this beautiful morning?" Amber asked.

"Santa came to my house and brought me some wonderful presents," Holly said.

"That's really nice," Amber said.

"Mommy, look at all the presents under this Christmas tree," Holly said.

"Well, before we open presents," Amber said, "we have to have breakfast. We're also waiting for Chris and Sapphire to come."

"Okay," Holly voiced, sounding a little disappointed.

"You wouldn't want to open presents without Sapphire, would you?" Amber said to Holly.

"No," Holly said.

"They'll be here soon, sweetie," Destiny said.

Just as they were about to sit to eat breakfast, Chris and Sapphire walked in.

"Merry Christmas, everyone," Chris said as Sapphire ran over to Holly and hugged her. He was holding three white Christmas roses— one for Destiny, one for Virginia, and one for his mother. He handed one to each of the women and kissed their cheeks.

"Merry Christmas, Sapphire!" Holly said as she hugged Sapphire back.

Suddenly, Paige walked through the door and apologized for being late. "I had a flat tire."

"Well, I'm glad you made it," Amber said.

"Hi, sweetheart," Daniel said as he kissed her cheek.

"Let's all enjoy a hearty breakfast," Eric said.

"Let's join hands, and Eric will offer a prayer on the food," Amber said.

"Dear Heavenly Father, we are blessed this morning to all be together to celebrate this holy day. We are so grateful for the birth of Jesus Chris and all that He has sacrificed for us. We love Him and give thanks for His guidance, love, and faith. We ask Thee for a blessing upon this food. May it nourish and strengthen our bodies so that we may do Thy will. Amen," Eric said.

Once breakfast was over, they all went into the living room.

Destiny went up and whispered a thank-you for the present.

"You're welcome, my dear," Chris said.

"Look at all those presents," Sapphire said.

Everyone sat on the furniture, while Eric put on his Santa hat and began to pass the presents out one by one. Holly was thrilled to get two more snow globes for her shelf, some new clothes, a carousel, some games, and toys. Sapphire received several little stuffed animals, some pajamas, clothes, puzzles, and toys. Both Sapphire and Holly also got the same beautiful red dress to wear for Christmas. They were very excited about that. Amber received a beautiful quilted blanket and a beautiful necklace. Eric got some tools for his shed and some new pants and shirts. Chris received a new carving set, some clothes, and a book. Destiny received some bridal magazines, a wedding planner, an artist painting set, a gold bracelet with her name on it, and some things for her house. Daniel received some new shirts and tie, along with a suit coat and some books. Daniel thought as he tried on the coat that he would look pretty sharp when he took Paige out for a date.

"I love your outfit. It's nice," Paige said to Daniel.

Paige received a new quilted blanket and some pretty jewelry. Virginia received a handmade quilt, some chocolates, and a book.

"You look so handsome in that suit," Destiny said.

"Thank you," Chris said. "It fits great, and it's very comfortable."

Everyone was so happy with their gifts. Once all the gifts were passed out, Sapphire and Holly unwrapped some of their toys and played with them.

"I love watching the expression on the girls' faces as they opened their presents. It's so precious," Destiny said.

"There's something magical about Christmas when you have children," Chris said.

Everyone helped clean up the living room, and then Chris and Destiny started to assemble a few of the toys the girls received.

"What a fun morning it has been," Paige said.

"You look so pretty today," Daniel said.

"Thank you," Paige replied.

The day was filled with joy and laughter. Everyone was enjoying Christmas Day.

Destiny and Chris started their wedding planning as they began looking through Destiny's bridal books and began to write some notes down.

"I think that I'll make a wedding planning board and cut out any of the ideas that we like in these books, Destiny said.

"Good idea," Chris said.

"Chris, who do you want as your best man?" Destiny asked.

"I think I'll ask Daniel," Chris said. "How about you? Who are you going to ask to be your maid of honor?" Chris asked.

"A lot of my friends live in Utah, so I think that I'll ask Paige. We have been becoming pretty close. I really like her," Destiny replied. "I will ask my mom if she will walk me down the aisle. I'm sure she'll be thrilled. What do you say that we have Sapphire and Holly as our flower girls?" Destiny asked.

"I love the idea!" Chris said. "We'll ask everyone after supper. Let the girls play," Chris said with a sweet kiss.

"I like the idea," Destiny said as she continued to look at the bridal magazine.

As the day went on, everyone was enjoying one another's company. In the late afternoon, many of the visitors staying at the B and B came inside to wish Amber and Eric a merry Christmas and to say how much they have enjoyed their stay at the B and B. Amber and Eric were so touched by their comments and happy that they enjoyed their stay.

When evening came, everyone gathered for supper and then sat in the living room as Destiny and Chris wanted to talk to everyone.

"Destiny and I have made some decisions about our wedding," Chris said.

"Daniel, it would be a great honor if you would be my best man."

"Wow, I didn't expect this," Daniel said. "But yes, I would be happy to be your best man," he said as he hugged his brother.

"Paige, would you be my maid of honor?" Destiny asked.

"Oh yes! I would love to," she said as she hugged Destiny.

"Mom, will you walk me down the aisle?"

Virginia had tears in her eyes thinking how much Destiny would have loved to have had her dad walk her down the aisle.

"Yes, Destiny, I will walk you down the aisle," her mother said. "I wish your father were here."

"I know, Mom," Destiny said as she hugged her mom.

"Your father would be so proud of you," Virginia said. "Your father and I have saved money for this day, so I can help you and Chris with the wedding."

"Thanks, Mom," Destiny and Chris said.

"We'll pitch in as well. You two are going to have a wonderful wedding," Amber said.

Lastly, talking to Sapphire and Holly, Destiny asked, "Would you two girls like to be the flower girls?"

"Yes! Yes!" the girls said as they jumped for joy.

"This is awesome!" Sapphire said.

"I can't wait," Holly said.

"Well, I should get home," Chris said.

"Aw, do we have to?" Sapphire said.

"Yes, we have to," Chris remarked as Sapphire went and hugged everyone a good night. "It's been a very busy day, and I have to work tomorrow," Chris said. "Paige will be watching you while you're on school vacation. Thanks, Mom and Dad, for the wonderful Christmas," Chris said.

"Yes, thank you," Destiny said as Holly went to hug everyone.

"Good night," Chris said to Daniel and Paige. "May I walk all of you out to your car?" Chris asked as he helped carry the presents to the car.

"That would be great," Destiny said. "Good night, everyone. Have a good evening," Destiny said as she hugged everyone goodbye.

"Good night," Virginia said.

Chris got Destiny all set in her car, and then he went and got his and Sapphire's gifts and put them into his truck.

"We have to get home and take care of Dakota."

"I miss Dakota," Sapphire said. "She's such a good dog."

"She'll be happy to see us," Chris said.

"You know what, Daddy," Sapphire said, "I'm so excited that I'm going to be a flower girl."

"It is very exciting!" Chris told Sapphire.

When Chris got home, he brought in the presents and took care of Dakota and then got Sapphire ready for bed.

"Did you have a nice Christmas?" Chris asked.

"Yes, I did," Sapphire said. "I love my family, and it's always nice to be with them."

"Well, little princess, it's time you hit the hay," Chris said as he read Sapphire a story and tucked her into bed.

"Merry Christmas, Daddy," Sapphire said.

"Merry Christmas to you too," Chris said.

When Destiny was bringing Holly home, Holly said in the car how excited she was to be in the wedding.

"You'll be a beautiful flower girl," Destiny said.

"Yes, you will," Virginia said.

"When are we going to get my dress?" Holly said.

"Soon, sweetie, soon," Destiny said.

When they all arrived home, Destiny put Holly to bed and read her a story.

"Mommy, thank you for the best Christmas ever," Holly said.

"It was a wonderful day," Destiny said as she snugged next to her, talking.

Virginia walked into Holly's bedroom and wished her sweet dreams and kissed her good night.

"Mommy, when you get married, where will we live?" Holly asked.

"We will move all of our things to Chris's house," Destiny said.

"My bed, my toys, my books, my dolls, my shelf, and my fairy mural?" Holly asked.

"Yes, everything, my dear," Destiny said. "Chris said that your new room can be painted the same color lavender as you have in your bedroom now."

"When can I call Chris daddy?" Holly asked.

"Once we get married," Destiny said. "Too many questions, my dear. It's time you get some sleep," Destiny to Holly.

"Good night, Mommy," Holly said with a kiss to her cheek.

"Good night. Sweet dreams," Destiny said with a kiss to her forehead.

The next morning, Destiny and Holly got up, had their breakfast, and then headed to the floral shop. Once Destiny got Holly started on her homework, she went to talk to her manager, Rose.

"Good morning, Rose," Destiny said.

"Good morning, Destiny," Rose said.

"How was your Christmas?" Destiny asked.

"It was wonderful," Rose told her. "And yours?"

"It was great!" Holly voiced. Destiny told Holly to get back to her schoolwork.

"Holly and I had a marvelous Christmas," Destiny told her.

"Destiny, you have a ring on finger?" Rose asked in excitement.

"On Christmas Eve, Chris proposed to me, and we're getting married on New Year's Eve," Destiny said.

"Then we better start planning your flower arrangements," Rose said.

"Do you know which flowers you would like for your wedding?" Rose asked.

"There are so many beautiful flowers," Destiny said.

"Let's start off with your favorite flower," Rose said.

"I love lavender roses and blue hydrangeas," Destiny said.

"Well, I think that you have narrowed down your bouquet," Rose said.

"How about if I add some white roses too? Some of the dainty stephanotis would be nice and some baby's breath to tuck into the bouquet," Destiny said.

"It sounds beautiful," Rose told her. "We can make them the day before New Year's Eve."

"I would like Paige, my maid of honor, to have a similar bouquet, just smaller. I would like the two flower girls to have a white basket filled with white rose petals to toss in church," Destiny said.

"How about your hair?" Rose asked. "Are you going to have a veil?"

"No," Destiny said. "I think that I would like a fragrant gardenia in my hair."

"Sounds so elegant," Rose said.

"Chris and Daniel, his best man, will have a single lavender rose boutonniere. His dad as well," Destiny said. "Oh, I almost forgot." Destiny continued. "I need two corsages, one for my mother and one for Chris's mother. The wedding is going to be for Chris and my family and some friends. For the reception, I would like to have a few lavender roses in vases for the tables."

"This sounds so elegant and romantic," Rose said. "I'll put the order in today, and we'll get them in plenty of time to make your bouquets."

Once all the wedding flowers were set, Destiny got back to work on the ordered floral arrangements for their customers. It was a lovely day, and Destiny was so excited to have begun the planning of the wedding. Destiny took a few days off from work so she could get some wedding preparations done.

Chapter 13

The next morning, Destiny, Virginia, Amber, Paige, and the two girls went shopping for dresses. The bridal shop downtown was the only one in town. As they entered the shop, everyone was welcomed.

"So who's the bride?" the bridal consultant asked.

"It's Destiny," Virginia said, pointing to her. "I'm her mom, Virginia, and this is her daughter, Holly. We also have Chris's mom, Amber, and his daughter, Sapphire, with us."

"What do you say that we start with the bride?" the consultant stated. "What type of dress are you looking for?"

"I will have to find something off the rack because I am getting married on New Year's Eve."

"Oh my!" the consultant remarked. "We have several dresses that you can look at in the back room."

"I'm looking for something with some lace and chiffon," Destiny said.

Everyone began looking at the wedding gowns. One gown after another, Destiny rejected. After an hour, she was beginning to get discouraged when she found the perfect dress. It was a beautiful white gown with a low top and white lace overlay up to her neck and short lace sleeves. The bottom of the gown was all chiffon.

"Try it on, Destiny," Virginia said. When Destiny came out of the dressing room, tears ran down everyone's cheeks. "You look stunning," Virginia said.

"Breathtaking," Amber said.

"Mommy, you look like an angel," Holly said.

"You look beautiful," Paige said.

"You look so pretty, Destiny," Sapphire told her.

When Destiny looked in the mirror, she thought that she looked just like a bride and felt wonderful about her choice. Tears filled her eyes.

"This is the one," Destiny told everyone as she twirled around in a circle, admiring her gown. Destiny also bought a pair of white shoes, gold earrings, and a dainty gold necklace with a single diamond in it. Once she took off the gown, the consultant hung the dress back on the hanger and stored away for Destiny. Destiny was lucky that the dress fit her perfectly and that no alterations were needed. Once Destiny was set, Amber and Virginia started looking for their gowns to try on. Virginia found a beautiful navy blue gown with embroidered flowers all along the front and sides of the gown. It was stunning. Amber found a navy blue gown with shades of blue beads on the front of the dress and chiffon flowing along the waist to the bottom of the gown. It was simply beautiful. Paige found a lavender chiffon gown with an embroidered top and flowing chiffon from the waist down. It was very pretty. Once they finished, it was the flower girls' turn.

Destiny had something in mind, but she was not sure she'd see it at the bridal shop. Destiny browsed through several racks of flower girl dresses. She finally found the dress that she saw in the bridal book. It was beautiful. It was a white floral top with a ballet-type skirt and ribbon that went around the waist. Each of the girls tried the dress on, and luckily, they had two of the same dress.

"I love this dress," Holly said. "It looks like a fairy dress."

"I love the dress too," Sapphire said as she touched the flowers on the dress.

"You two girls look absolutely beautiful," Destiny said.

"Like little angels," Virginia said.

"It's a perfect dress for them, "Amber said.

"You two look so pretty in those dresses," Paige said. "I wonder if they have it in my size."

"You're so funny," Sapphire said as everyone laughed.

"Thank you for all your help," Destiny said to the dress consultant. "I'll be back to get the gowns."

"Now that we have all the dresses set, why don't we go out for lunch and then go look at wedding cakes?" Virginia said.

"Well, Chris, and I wanted to do that," Destiny said.

"We can just look at them, and then you and Chris can come down to do the cake testing," Amber said.

"Okay, I guess that will be all right," Destiny said.

After lunch, all the ladies went to the bakery to check out the cakes.

"There are so many types of cakes," Destiny said as she looked through the wedding cake book.

"What type of wedding cake are you looking for?" the baker asked.

"I think that I want a simple three-layer cake with lavender and white roses," Destiny said.

"What flavor?" the baker asked.

"I'll be back with Chris to decide on the flavor."

When everyone was done looking at wedding cakes, they chose a dessert to sit down and enjoy.

"Let's head back to the bed-and-breakfast," Amber said. "Chris is going to get Sapphire after work."

Everyone climbed in Amber's SUV and headed back to her home.

While waiting for Chris, Virginia and Amber sat down with Destiny to discuss the wedding reception menu.

"Have you and Chris talked about the reception?" Virginia asked.

"There's a restaurant called the Cabin in the Woods. Chris recommended it," Destiny said. "We were lucky that there was a cancellation and we were able to get New Year's Eve booked there. We're also getting married at your family church," she told Amber.

"How lovely," Amber remarked.

"Since the wedding is going to be fairly small with about fifty people, Chris and I thought that we would have a local band come and play some lively music," Destiny said. "If you would like to choose the reception menu for us, we'd like that. You know what Chris and I like to eat," Destiny added. "Hey, Chris's truck just pulled up," Destiny said.

"Hi, ladies," Chris said. "How are the wedding plans coming?"

"We all have our dresses, and we checked some wedding cakes out."

"Wait till you see Destiny in her wedding gown," Amber said. "She is exquisite."

"I'm sure she is," Chris said as he bent over to Destiny for a kiss.

"Do you want to go back to the bakery and choose our wedding cake?" Destiny asked Chris.

"Mom, can Sapphire stay and play with me?" Holly asked.

"Sure, Virginia and I have some work to do anyway for the reception," Amber said. "We'll keep an eye on them."

Destiny and Chris went to the bakery. The baker recognized Destiny and offered them a seat at the table.

"I told them that I wanted a simple cake, nothing to elaborate. Some lavender and white roses," Destiny said.

"That sounds really pretty," Chris said.

"I will go and cut up some different types of cakes for you to choose from," the barker said.

The baker brought out a lemon chiffon cake, a triple berry cream cheesecake, a dark chocolate, a red velvet cake, a white chocolate with raspberry, a coconut and lime cake, a carrot cake, and a vanilla cake.

"Oh my goodness! How do we choose?" Destiny asked.

"One bite at a time," Chris said jokingly. "I have an idea. Why not choose three varieties of our favorite cake and have one flavor for each of the layers?" Chris asked.

"Okay," Destiny replied.

"Let the tasting begin," Chris said.

"They are all so good," Destiny said.

"Yes, they are," Chris said.

After tasting all the cakes, Chris and Destiny choose the dark chocolate cake, the coconut and lime cake, and the white chocolate with raspberry cake for their wedding cake.

"This was a nice way to end our day," Destiny said.

"Eating dessert is always a good time." Chris chuckled. "Tomorrow do you want to go and talk to the bishop about our wedding?"

"Sure, that would be wonderful!" Destiny answered. "Then we can go to the town clerk to get our marriage license."

"Just think in less than a week, you will become my wife," Chris said as he kissed Destiny.

"It is coming fast, Chris," Destiny said, hugging him. "I can't wait."

"Let's head back to the B and B for the girls. I am really pumped for the day I become your husband," Chris said.

"My husband," Destiny said. "It has a good ring to it," she said with a smile.

"Speaking of rings, we need to do that too," Chris said.

"Why don't we go and look at the rings after we see the bishop?" Destiny asked.

"We can't forget the marriage license," Chris said.

"Sounds good," Destiny said. "We'd better get home to see the girls. It'll be another busy day tomorrow."

Once they got back to the B and B, Chris and Destiny got the girls, and then each headed home. Next morning, Destiny brought Holly over to Chris's house to play with Sapphire. Paige had kindly offered to watch both girls. After breakfast, Chris and Destiny drove together to see the bishop. He was a nice man with a big heart.

"Good morning, Chris," Bishop Irving said. "Who is this lovely lady?"

"This is my lovely bride-to-be, Destiny," Chris said.

"Nice to meet you," the bishop said.

"It's nice to meet you too," Destiny said.

"Now let's go over the wedding plans," the bishop said.

The meeting went well, and Chris and Destiny got everything that they asked for in the ceremony. They were very happy.

"Thank you for all your help," Chris said as he shook the bishop's hand.

"I look forward to your ceremony," Bishop Irving said.

"It was nice meeting you," Destiny told the bishop as she shook his hand and smiled.

"Let's head out to the town hall," Chris said.

"I'm so excited! Let's go!" Destiny said.

So off to the town hall, and within a few minutes, they had their marriage license.

"Time is flying by, so we better go and look at the rings before they close," Chris said.

"Let's go!" Destiny said.

When Destiny and Chris got to the jewelry store, they looked at a variety of gold wedding bands. Chris decided on a simple gold band. Destiny chose a floral pink-gold band that would look nice with her engagement ring.

"I can't wait to place this wedding ring on your finger," Chris said as he tried the band on her finger.

"I can't either. It will be a special day," Destiny said. "We're lucky that we found the rings so quickly. I was a little nervous about it."

"If we didn't find one here, then there's another jewelry store we would have gone to in the next town," Chris said. "All that matters to me is that you're happy with your ring."

"I love my wedding ring!" Destiny said.

"Time to head back to my house. Paige told me that she has another date with Daniel, and I don't want to make her stay too late."

When they got back to Chris's house, Sapphire and Holly were playing dress up.

"I remember when I was a child and used to dress up too," Destiny said.

"We're going to have a fashion show, so have a seat," Sapphire said, talking to Chris and Destiny.

One by one, each of the two girls showed off their fancy outfits, walking down the hallway, spinning around, and gracefully walking past them. It was a lot of fun.

"My beauties," Chris said, cheering them on.

"You're beautiful!" Destiny told them.

Chris looked at his clock and realized it was getting late. "Now that the dress show is over, it's time you get your pajamas on."

"Holly, you need to get your regular clothes back on so we can go home." "Thanks for the lovely day, Chris," Destiny said.

"You're welcome," Chris said.

Destiny brought Holly to the B and B to check on the ladies doing the wedding menu.

"I hope you ladies had a pleasant day," Destiny told her mother and Amber.

"We have the food menu complete," Amber said.

"That's great!" Destiny said.

"You'll be really happy with what we picked," Virginia said. "We chose fresh rolls with whipped butter, fresh fruit cups, garden salad, mashed Yukon gold potatoes, and honey-glazed baby carrots and green beans. People can decide on which meat or fish they want from prime rib, glazed chicken, or baked haddock."

"This sounds great!" Destiny said.

"How did your day go with getting all those errands done?"

"Good. We got our marriage license, our wedding bands, and we spoke to Bishop Irving," Destiny said.

"Well, it sounds like you had a very busy day, and we should head home so you can get some rest," Virginia said. "And I'll even drive."

"Thanks, Mom," Destiny said tiredly.

"Weddings will do that to you," Amber said. "Good night, ladies," Amber added.

"Good night," Destiny said with a smile.

In the morning of the next day, Destiny called Chris to see if he wanted to go and look at tuxedos after work.

"It sounds like a good idea," Chris said. "But I need to bring Daniel and my father too."

"Of course," Destiny said. "Daniel can bring Paige if he would like to."

"I'll call Daniel and my father right now," Chris said. "Talk to you later, sweetheart."

"Hey, Daniel, would you like the come with Destiny and me to look at tuxedos?"

"Well, I have a date with Paige, so if you don't mind if I bring her too, I'd be happy to go," Daniel said.

"Great. Then I'll see you six o'clock," Chris said. "Let me talk to Dad," Chris said to Daniel. "Hey, Dad, would you want to go and get your tuxedo today?"

"I think your mother has something planned," Eric said. "I'll get back to you."

Once the workday was over, Chris brought Sapphire to see her grandmother. Destiny was on her way to the B and B with Holly. When they got there, Amber was gone.

"Amber went to her friend's birthday party, so she has put me in charge of the girls," Eric said. "Don't you two worry. We'll have a great time."

"We'll have to make it another time to get your tuxedo," Chris said to his dad. Daniel and Paige had just arrived after having a nice dinner out.

"Now that we're all here, let's go!" Daniel said.

They all piled in Destiny's Mustang and headed out to the bridal shop.

"I'd love to see your wedding dress on you tonight, Destiny," Chris said.

"Oh no, you can't. It's bad luck to see my dress before the wedding," Destiny replied.

"Just kidding. I knew that," Chris said, laughing.

"You tease!" Destiny said. "We're just going to look at tuxedos."

When they all arrived at the bridal shop, they began to look through the men's catalog to see what type of tuxedo they wanted.

"I like this style," Chris said.

"I like it too," Daniel said. "Let's try them on. It makes me look like a supermodel."

"Don't mind Daniel. He does think very highly of his appearance," Paige voiced. "Though he does look really handsome in that suit."

As Chris tried his tuxedo on, Destiny helped him with his collar. "You look like a groom," Destiny said with a smile. "Very handsome."

"Thanks, babe. I feel like one too," Chris said.

Chris let the tailor know that the wedding was going to be a New Year's Eve wedding.

"Don't worry, I have all the tuxedos ready for you," he told Chris.

"I'll be back soon with my father to order his tux," Chris said.

Once the tailor took the men's measurements, they were all set and headed back to the B and B.

"Okay, so that's done," Destiny said. "I think all we have left to do after we get your dad's tux is to make the wedding invitations. They had some at the bridal shop, but I think that I'm just going to make them off the computer," Destiny said.

"Great idea!" Chris told Destiny.

"I think that I'll wait till tomorrow when I'm more awake. It's been another busy day," Destiny said.

"I'm glad that it didn't take too long," Chris said. "I want to get back to Sapphire. The girls have probably tired my dad out by now."

When they walked into the B and B, Chris's dad was playing a game with the girls.

"Hey, Dad, how did tonight go?" Chris asked.

"Everything went fine," Eric said. "I think that the girls had a good time with their old grandpa."

"It was fun playing with Grandpa," Sapphire said.

"I had fun too," Holly said, "especially when we had an ice cream sundae."

"Thanks for coming, Daniel and Paige," Chris told them.

The girls were getting tired, so Chris and Destiny each brought them home.

The next morning, Destiny got up early to make the invitations before going to work. She sat at the computer and began to design a border, color, and font that she wanted to use.

Talking to herself, she said, "Since the wedding has a lot of lavender, I think that I'll make them white with a lavender border, a black inscription, and a white ribbon tied to the top of the invitation." It gave Destiny a good feeling knowing that she could design an invitation for their wedding. Placing all the detailed information on the card made everything seem real. It made her smile.

When Holly woke up, Destiny had just finished the invitations. Now she just had to print them out. Holly went in to see her mom at the computer. She glanced at an invitation and told her mom that they were very pretty.

"All done," Destiny said. "I just have to send Chris a snapshot of the invitation. Now let's go make some breakfast."

"Can we have pancakes?" Holly asked.

"Sure. Then we need to get dressed and head down to the florist," Destiny said.

Later that day, Chris sent Destiny a text message that he loved the invitations that she made.

Days were going by fast, and the wedding was only a few days away. Invitations were sent out, and about fifty people responded and were coming to the wedding. Destiny and Holly went down to the bridal shop and picked up all the gowns and the girls' dresses. It was a nice day to get all the final touches for the wedding done. When Destiny got home, she tried her wedding gown on one more time before the wedding. As she looked in the mirror, all she could think of was the day she would marry Chris. She felt so elegant and pretty in her gown. She even played with her hair, trying to come up with some type of pretty hairstyle.

"Mommy, you look so pretty," Holly said.

"Thank you, sweetie," Destiny told her. "Let's try on your dress now." As they both stood looking in the mirror, Destiny felt such joy. "This is a day I will always cherish with you, Holly," she said.

The next morning, Destiny went to work to check in all her flowers ordered for the wedding. She was very happy that all her flowers had arrived. Destiny got Holly situated with her schoolwork, and then she and Rose started to work on the bouquets and corsages. An hour later, they were all done.

"I love the way the flowers came out," Destiny told Rose.

"I especially love your bouquet. It's so perfect for you," Rose said with a smile.

"Let's put them all back in the cooler," Destiny said.

When the day was over, Destiny and Holly went home.

"Mommy, let's call Chris and see what he is doing," Holly said.

"That's a great idea," Destiny told her.

"Hi, Chris," Destiny said. "What are you and Sapphire up to tonight?"

"Just hanging out with my girl," Chris replied.

"Why don't you two come over to my house?" Destiny asked.

"Sounds good," Destiny said. "See you in a bit."

"Feel free to bring Dakota. I'd love to see her."

When they arrived at Destiny's house, Destiny and Holly were playing cards. Dakota ran inside and wagged her tail and wanted attention from Destiny and Holly.

"You're such a good girl," Destiny said, patting her.

"Hi, Dakota," Holly said as she hugged her.

"I'm glad that you two are here," Destiny said.

"Why don't we have a relaxing evening with a movie and some popcorn?" Destiny asked.

"I like that idea," Chris said.

"So what kind of movie does everyone want?" Chris asked.

"An animation movie!" Sapphire said.

Destiny went and made the popcorn, while Chris got some drinks.

"After all the crazy, busy days of planning this wedding, it feels good to just do nothing and relax," Destiny said. "I loved every minute of it though."

Once the movie was over, Chris and Sapphire went home with Dakota.

The next morning, Chris went down to the bridal shop with Eric so he could get measured for a tux. Lucky for Eric, they had a tuxedo his size, so he was able to take his with him. While Chris was there, he picked up his and Daniel's tuxedos. Then he picked up some flowers at the florist for Destiny.

That afternoon was the wedding rehearsal at the church. It was going to be fun to practice for the big day. When they all arrived at the church, Bishop Irving was getting ready to walk them through the ceremony rehearsal. Destiny and Chris were kind of nervous but silly during the practice. "I guess that happens to all couples," Destiny said. After practice, everyone went out to celebrate the rehearsal dinner at an Italian restaurant.

"I have had the best night tonight, and I'm looking forward to the wedding tomorrow," Amber said.

"What a wonderful evening," Eric said. "I am so proud of the both of you."

"Now before we leave, Chris, you have to say good night to Destiny because you can't see her until the wedding," Virginia said.

"What a bummer," Chris said.

"You don't want me to have bags under my eyes, do you?" Destiny said jokingly.

It was the night before the wedding, so Chris knew that he couldn't see the bride before they were to be married, but it was hard.

"I would like it if Sapphire could sleep over my house so I can get her ready for the wedding," Destiny said.

"Sure, that would be fine with me," Chris said.

"I'll be there in the late afternoon to help you so you can be ready by five thirty," Amber said to Destiny.

On the way home, Chris called Destiny.

"Hi, babe. How excited are you?" Chris said.

"I have butterflies in my stomach, but I'm so excited," Destiny said.

"Yeah, me too," Chris said.

"I can't believe that it's here and tomorrow I'll be your wife," Destiny said.

"I know," Chris said. "It's great to be getting married on New Year's Eve."

"It is," Destiny replied. "I hope when we leave the church that evening, the northern lights will be in the sky," Destiny said.

"That would be awesome!" Chris said. "Well, I think that I should go and spent some time with Sapphire and Dakota," Chris said. "I love you, Destiny."

"I love you too, Chris!"

Chapter 14

The morning arrived, the day of the wedding. Destiny, Holly, Sapphire, and Virginia got up and started their day. It was a relaxing morning, just being together and enjoying one another's company. Sapphire and Holly colored for a bit and then played with Holly's dolls.

"I thought that I would be a nervous wreck, but I feel calm and happy," Destiny said to her mother.

"That's because you know it's right," Virginia said. "I have something for you, Destiny, that I have been saving since you were a little girl."

"What is it?" she asked.

Virginia handed her a box, and Destiny opened it. It was a beautiful charm bracelet with a blue gem and Destiny's name engraved on it.

"It's a bracelet your father picked out for you for when you got married. He'd be so proud if you would wear it today."

"There's my something blue that I needed, and of course, I will wear it," Destiny said with tears in her eyes.

"Your father is here in spirit," Virginia said as she hugged Destiny.

"You and dad have always been there for me, and I'm so blessed to have you in my life," Destiny said.

"Now no crying. You don't want swollen eyes," Virginia said.

As Destiny wiped the tears in her eyes, Holly came into the bedroom.

"Holly, look at what my father got me," Destiny said. "Grandma has been saving it for me all these years, and now I'm going to wear it on my wedding day. I'll always treasure it. Thanks, Mom."

As evening was approaching fast, Destiny decided that it was time to get dressed. Amber had now arrived and was helping Virginia get Destiny dressed into her wedding gown.

Once she was dressed, Amber got Holly and Sapphire into their dresses, and the mothers both got their gowns on. Next was hair and makeup. Virginia helped Destiny with her hair and makeup, and then Destiny helped her mom with her hair and makeup. Then Virginia took care of Holly's hair. Amber was taking care of her own hair and makeup and then Sapphire's hair. Just as they finished their hair, the flowers arrived.

"Now that I have my flowers, I am ready to become Mrs. Destiny Adams," Destiny voiced.

Once all the ladies were ready, they hopped into a reindeer-drawn sleigh and headed for the church to be there a little before six o'clock.

Chris was having a crazy morning with Daniel and Eric. They must have stayed up most of the night talking. But they did compose themselves and got ready for the wedding. When Chris, Daniel, and Eric were ready, they headed for the church.

When Chris, Daniel, and Eric arrived at the church, Rose walked in with their boutonnieres. She helped them put the flower on their lapels. Once situated, Chris, Daniel, and Eric greeted the guests as they arrived. The church looked so beautiful with the flowers surrounding the altar and pews. As the time came closer, Chris and Daniel rolled out the white paper liner down the aisle for Destiny. Chris and Daniel went up to the altar and waited for the wedding to begin. Suddenly, the music began as the church doors opened. Paige walked down the aisle. She looked radiant. Daniel smiled as she got closer to the altar. Then Sapphire and Holly came down the aisle in their precious little flower girl dresses. The girls tossed rose petals on the floor. It was very sweet. Once the girls got closer to Chris, he walked over to the pew to get some white roses that were set up for him. Chris handed one flower to Sapphire and one to Holly. He kissed their cheeks and then helped them to their seats.

As the music changed to the wedding march, Destiny came out from behind the door. Destiny entered the church with her mother in arm, glowing with beauty and elegance. They walked down the aisle smiling as they passed each guest, and then her eyes met Chris's. The moment seemed to freeze in time as she only saw Chris. As she walked closer to Chris, he gently took her hand and led her up to the altar. Destiny handed her bouquet to Paige, and the ceremony began. Chris and Destiny then walked over where the roses were and passed one out to their mothers and then gave them each a kiss. Once on the altar, the bishop said some words.

"It is a beautiful day, one that we unite two people in love. Chris and Destiny welcome you and thank you for coming. Chris and Destiny have asked that we start off with the uniting of two families."

Chris and Destiny waved to Sapphire and Holly to come up to the altar. Each of them lit a candle and then join all together to light the unity candle symbolizing the unity of becoming one family. Then the girls each took a seat.

"Chris and Destiny," Bishop Irving said, "have decided to write their own vows. Chris, you will go first."

Daniel handed Chris and Destiny their wedding bands as they said their vows.

"Destiny, my love, today I take you as my wife. It is with great joy that I have you by my side. The day I met you, I saw something so special in you, and with each day, my love for you became stronger. I have a special place in my heart to hold you near, a place where our love can grow each day. As we begin this journey, I vow to love you, honor you, respect you, and be true to you. I will always cherish this day as you become my wife and we become one family," Chris said as he placed Destiny's wedding band on her finger.

"Destiny, it's your turn to say your vows," Bishop Irving said.

"Chris, I am the happiest woman in the world as you become my husband. I am humbled by your love, goodness, and kind spirit. I love you more with each passing day. My heart is full as our two families become one. I pledge to love you, honor you, and be your loving wife," Destiny said as she placed Chris's wedding band on his finger.

"It is with great pleasure that I now pronounce you husband and wife," Bishop Irving said. "You may kiss the bride."

It was a beautiful moment as they shared their first kiss as husband and wife. Everyone cheered. It was a beautiful ceremony.

Once the ceremony was over, Chris and Destiny, along with the rest of the wedding party, stood in a line for people to congratulate them. Then it was off for formal wedding pictures. Just as they left the church, Destiny looked up and saw the northern lights. She was so happy. The photographer took several pictures with the northern lights as the background. The sky was swirling in greens and purples, a perfect backdrop for the pictures. While photos were being taken, the guests drove to the Cabin in the Woods restaurant. It didn't take long before the bridal party was at the restaurant too. The wedding party all lined up as each couple entered the restaurant. Cheers were followed as each person came into the room. Everyone clapped and cheered when Chris and Destiny were announced as Mr. and Mrs. Chris Adams. Smiles were on everyone's faces and loud cheers. It was such a happy time for all. When they got to their table and sat, Daniel offered a toast.

With a glass raised in the air, he said, "To Destiny and Chris, may you always find joy and happiness as you embark on this marvelous journey. May you find peace and harmony in your marriage with every twist and turn, and may you walk on the same path. I love you! Congratulations!"

Everyone drank their toast. Daniel also said a toast for Sapphire and Holly. "To my sweet angels, may you rejoice in being one family. May you always be happy with your life. And if your parents start to drive you crazy, just give me a call. I love you both, and I am so proud of you." Everyone said cheers and drank their toast.

The reception was a fun evening, and the bride and groom did their typical ceremonial events, such as Destiny and Chris's first dance; tossing of the bouquet, which Paige caught; tossing the garter, which Daniel caught; and the cutting of the cake.

It was a wonderful day as two families were united in love and a dream came true.